IMPERFECT

IN A SMALL TOWN

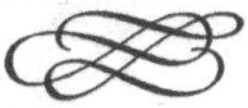

ALIE GARNETT

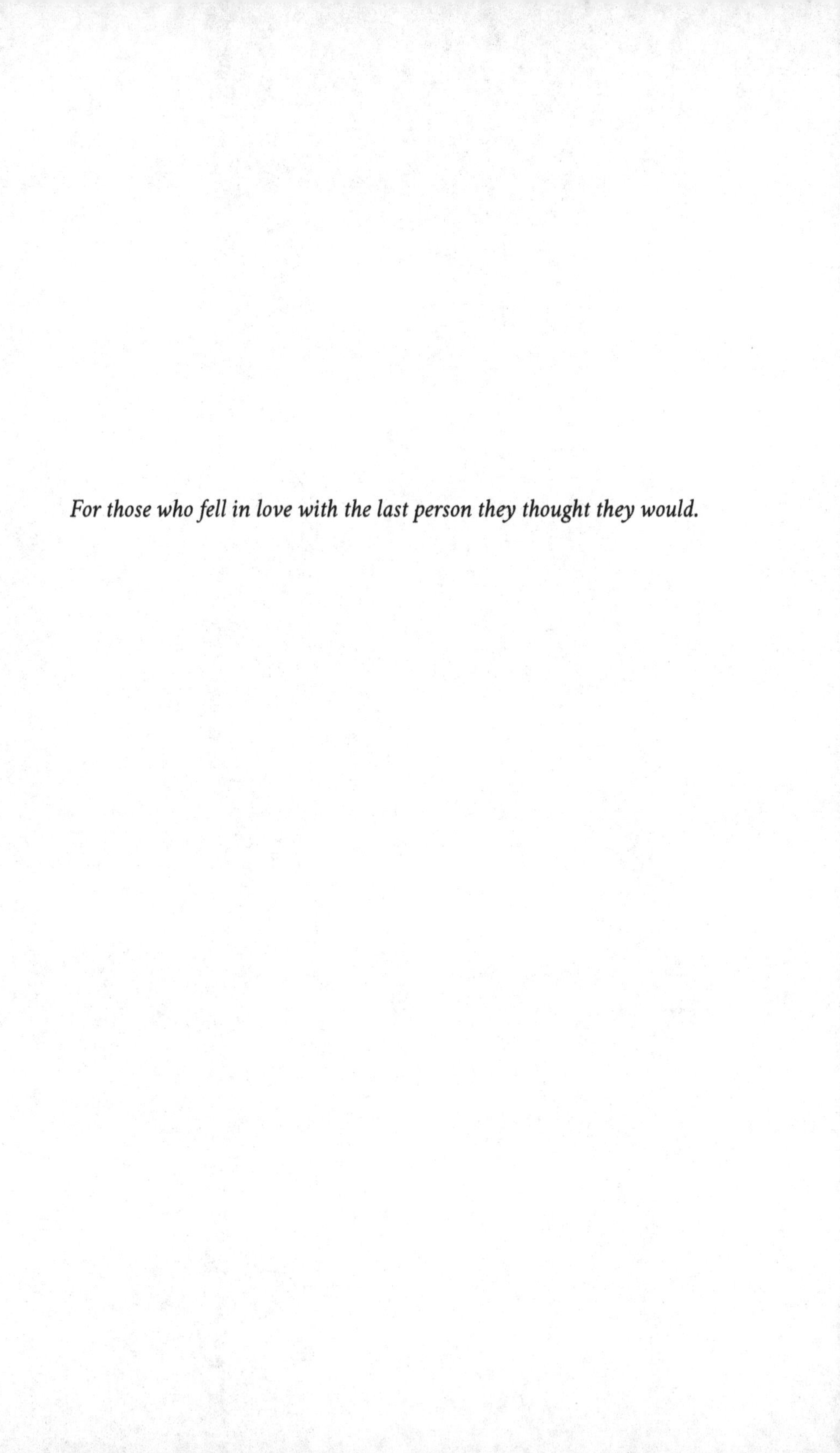

For those who fell in love with the last person they thought they would.

CHAPTER 1

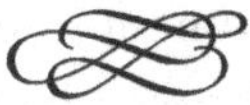

AMANDA NORDSKOV WAS TRAPPED in some kind of hell.

A personal hell because everyone around her was happy. Excited, even. At least nobody noticed, since nobody was even aware she wanted to be anywhere but in this room—with these people who she loved and who loved her.

Looking around the room that held her parents, her little sister Kit, Hue Strong, her brother's best friend, her brother, and his girl-friend, she could spend every day all day with these people. These people were not the person causing her so much pain. That pain was reserved for the tiny new baby in her brother's arms, and she was only a few hours old.

A baby. A living, breathing baby. Not that she hadn't seen babies every day when she was an OB nurse; she had, and it hadn't bothered her one bit. In fact, this baby wouldn't bother her either if it had been born last month or next month, but this month, this day, seeing a new baby was killing her.

Because today Amanda was exactly twenty weeks pregnant, but no one in the room knew or even suspected. And if she had her way, they never would. It hurt her that she could not share her news with everyone she loved, like her brother and sisters had over the years.

But in the end, when the pregnancy ended, as they always did, she didn't want the pity she always felt when they knew. Her pregnancies never ended in this room with family and friends smiling and talking about names, diapers, and who the baby looked like. Hers ended weeks too soon for anything to be done to save the baby she so badly wanted. Hers ended with her alone and in sorrow.

So today, as she welcomed her newest niece into her life, she steeled her heart for the moment the baby she carried was lost. Because after nine pregnancies, she had yet to have this moment. It was only a matter of time before this baby was also gone.

"Mandy, do you want to hold her?" Her brother Math smiled at her, a smile that hadn't dimmed since she had walked into the room. You would think it was his first kid, not fourth, by how excited he was. Maybe it was because it was his first with Tess that made this one a little more special. Finding the love of your life will do that to you.

Taking a deep breath, she said, "No, I think I'm coming down with something." She rubbed her neck as if it was bothering her.

"Are you sure? You're the baby person." Math shifted the baby her way. It was true she loved babies. Since her mom had brought home Mathias when she was almost three, she had loved babies. But today, she couldn't do it. Not today.

"Kit?" Her brother moved on to her sister beside her.

Amanda glanced over at her younger sister, who was a taller, slimmer version of herself. Other than their body type, they looked alike, from their blonde hair to their blue eyes. Even their noses were the same. Everything, except Kit's extra five inches.

"I already have one." The woman shifted her six-month-old in her arms. Kit was lucky to be the mother of five happy, healthy boys. At thirty, she was currently single and a history teacher in Grand Forks, the town they were currently in. Until last winter, Amanda had also been living in Grand Forks—a town considered large compared to the small town she had grown up in—but anything was large compared to Landstad. It was there she was the lone nurse practitioner at the town's lone new health clinic. A job she loved.

"Hue?" Math asked his best friend since kindergarten, maybe

before. Amanda couldn't remember not knowing him. Hubert Strong had been there for every big event in her brother's life, and this was no different. He was like another little brother to her.

"I'm good." The man held up his hands, as if to show them off.

Turning toward him in surprise, she saw the pain and despair in his blue eyes. Gasping slightly at his expression, she met his eyes when the sound made him look at her. Why was Hue hurting, looking at the baby? The man was a big, tough cop, after all.

Eyes back to the tiny baby, she watched her own mom take her from her son's arms with delight. Though the woman had already held the baby, she was willing to have another shot. Amanda had always known she got her love of babies from her mom.

That and her shortness, as she and her mom were the shortest in the family. But all the Nordskov kids got their coloring from her: the same blond hair and blue eyes. What her siblings were lucky not to have inherited was her mother's hips and her inability to lose weight. Since they all reached adulthood, she had felt small and round when her younger siblings were visiting.

"Mandy, I know you want to go next. You most likely don't have anything," Tess said from the hospital bed. Even after spending most of the day in labor, the woman looked refreshed and put together. She wasn't even wearing a hospital gown, but a tunic that perfectly matched her gray eyes.

Tess Thorn was Amanda's friend. She even considered her a close friend and had been that way for a bit longer than Tess had been dating her brother. Tess was the president of the only bank in Land-stad, and Math had spent months hating her until she ended up pregnant with his baby. Amanda knew some of the details, and that was enough. After all, he was her brother.

Even with her questionable taste in men, Amanda had gotten along with Tess, even more since the other woman had moved in with Math a few months before. It helped that Tess possessed the same dry sense of humor she did and that she was willing to put her brother in his place. Something a sister could appreciate.

"No, I really shouldn't. I actually think I shouldn't be in the same room if I'm coming down with something. I should just go." Faking a cough, she started to back toward the door behind her, hoping nobody asked what she had, because she had no illness to back up her lie. Just an uncontrollable need to flee this room.

"Mandy, you rode with us." Her mom barely looked up from the baby as she reminded Mandy.

Just her luck; she had ridden with her parents. At the time, it was nice to be able to catch a cat nap on the almost two-hour drive. Now she was regretting it. Though the nap had been so needed after a day that started before four with Math's panicked call that his girlfriend was in labor. Mandy couldn't understand her brother at all—this was his fourth kid. If anyone should be nervous, it was Tess. Except she was perfectly calm as she told her boyfriend everything they had already planned.

Not letting that deter her, Mandy continued back toward the door but ran into something hard and warm. It had to be Hue. Everyone else was in front of her, half of whom were watching her trying to leave.

Hue put his hands on her shoulders to steady her as his deep voice came over her shoulder. "I can take her home, Mrs. Nordskov. I was going to head out, anyway."

Everybody seemed okay with the idea as they said goodbye to them while Hue held her shoulders. His grasp was light but made a warm sensation spread through her body. The sensation almost had her lean back into him. Then his hands moved from her shoulder down her back as he turned her and steered her out of the room, away from the happy family moment she should want to be a part of but didn't have the strength for today.

"Let's get out of here," he said low enough that only she could hear him.

With his hand still on her back, he pushed her down the hallway faster than her shorter legs could move. As they moved past the nurses' station, she waved to some of her old co-workers she had chatted with on the way in, stalling before having to see the baby. The healthy, breathing baby.

Letting Hue navigate them through the hospital, she had no strength to tell him he was going too fast until she stumbled. She would have hit the floor if he hadn't caught her and steadied her. The action made him finally stop.

His arms were still holding her waist as she stood panting for air. She needed to exercise more since she was very obviously completely out of shape, or maybe he took her breath away with how good looking he was in those tight blue jeans and soft gray flannel he wore beneath his bulky jacket.

"Are you okay?" Hue was looking down at her, still holding her around the waist.

He had to be over six feet, she realized. *When had he gotten so tall?* she wondered as she looked up at him. Of course, he had been taller than her for over twenty years. She was thirty-six, and he was her brother's age at close to thirty-four, and he had probably outgrown her by the time he was fifteen. Maybe she hadn't stood close enough to him that she had to look up to him.

Over the last twenty years, she had seen him hundreds of times. Weddings, funerals, her brother's kids' birthdays, random gatherings, and football parties. In fact, she had been to more gatherings with him than without him. But until the summer before she moved home, he was always with his wife, Krystal, and Amanda had never been able to stand that woman.

Now she saw him even more regularly than before. He was her neighbor, her only neighbor in the apartment above her clinic. They even got together alone to watch sports on the weekends when they were both free but nobody else was. He was like another brother to her, always had been.

Not answering the question, she said, "Thank you. I needed out of there."

"Me too." He let go of her waist but took her hand and walked slower this time. He must have realized that she wasn't able to keep up with him.

Amanda wondered if he thought that she was fat after holding her around the waist. She had always been thicker, but with the pregnancy, she was even more so. Why did she suddenly care what Hue thought of her? It didn't matter what he thought of her weight—it didn't matter what anyone thought.

Once out the hospital doors, Amanda saw that it was snowing lightly. Feeling the cold flakes melt on her face made her feel better. She loved winter and all the snow and cold it brought. Summer was hot and windy. Winter was her season. It was November in North Dakota, and snow was not unusual in the early days of the month—it usually just melted as it hit the ground. That was what it was doing today.

Getting into Hue's red pickup, she was thankful to be out of the hospital and on her way home. Another few minutes might have broken her. Her emotions were frayed as it was.

"Do you want to grab something to eat before we leave town?" Hue asked as he pulled out of the parking lot. Landstad was two hours away, with nowhere to eat between the two towns.

"No," she said. She just wanted to get home, curl up in bed, and cry. But knowing if she didn't eat, she would be sick, she changed her mind. "Yes. I think I need something."

"Sit-down or fast food?" Hue didn't look at her as he drove.

"A drive-through is fine, unless you want to sit," she answered, then demanded herself to be polite. He was driving, it was his choice, but she hoped he opted for fast food.

"Fast food," he agreed.

By the time they were leaving town, they each had a burger, fries, and a pop for the trip. Glancing over at him as she ate a fry, she decided he turned out pretty good for the skinny red-haired kid she tutored in science in high school. He had filled out nicely with broad shoulders and muscles he'd not had back then. Though he still had the red hair, it was a darker shade now and looked really good when it was a little longer than it should be, like now.

He must have noticed she was looking at him because he turned to her and raised an eyebrow in question. In response, she threw a fry at him that bounced off his chest. Picking it up from his lap, he tossed it in his mouth with a grin as he chewed. "What went on in there, Nordskov?"

Taking a bite of her sandwich so she couldn't answer his question, she realized he always called her by her last name. Ever since she had returned to town, he hadn't called her Amanda or Mandy or any other nickname. Just Nordskov. Swallowing, she said, "I could ask you the same thing, Hue. What went on it there?"

"I don't do babies," he informed her.

"Me neither," she lied.

"I think the first time I met you, you had a baby in your arms."

"Probably Kit. She was born when I was six." Shrugging, she didn't even remember that day, but he was probably right.

"And you work with babies all the time," he reminded her, because they knew too much about each other.

"I don't know. Just couldn't today, that's all." She hoped it was enough of an explanation.

"Why didn't you and Seth have any kids?" His words made her choke on her fry.

At her coughing, he started pounding on her back, more like shoulder, because her back was resting on the seat back. "Sorry, I shouldn't have asked. That was too personal."

Taking a drink of her pop, she countered, "Why didn't you and Krystal?"

"Fertility issues. It just didn't happen." He looked back out the windshield at the landscape. They had been married for over a dozen years when the marriage broke. Amanda had never heard the reason behind it, but it may be that she didn't ask. She didn't pry into everyone's lives.

Or maybe she was happy Hue was finally free of that woman—the reasons behind it didn't matter. It hadn't helped that all of her siblings felt the same way. Krystal had been a piece of work.

"Did you see doctors?" she asked automatically. For years, she had worked with couples who had issues getting pregnant. It had been her job.

He nodded without looking at her. "Yup, many. We never got close."

"Is that why you got divorced?" she pried, because she wanted to know.

"Yup. She wanted kids. I couldn't give her that." His jovialness was gone from just minutes before.

"That's shitty." Amanda put her hand on his leg for support. But all it did was make her realize how firm and warm his leg was. Did he have muscles everywhere?

"Yes, it is." He glanced at her hand on his leg.

Self-consciously, she pulled her hand back because it was a little too nice to touch his leg. She looked over at him. "I am unable to carry a pregnancy to term. I lose them before twenty weeks."

She wasn't an expert on miscarriage just because of her job. At this point, she used to deal with women who had them all the time at work, and she has had nine herself. But she hated talking about hers.

"That sucks. Is that why Seth left you?"

"No, he left me because I worked too many nights, and his buddy's wife didn't. But at least they're still together and have a kid now." She bit into her sandwich, hoping that would stop her from talking. Her divorce was a lot older than his was, so it shouldn't still bother her. But it did. She saw it as a failure, after all.

Hue reached over and squeezed her shoulder. "No wonder we both just needed to get out of that room. Cute baby, though."

"Very cute. I had hoped she would look more like Tess than she does." Maybe it was because she still loved to see her brother lose, and that included in the gene pool. Being a big sister never ended.

"What do I always hear, Nordskov's breed true?" He grinned as he ate a fry, the tension broken.

That made her laugh out loud. It was a saying her dad would say when he looked at his now twelve grandchildren that all looked the same: blond-haired, blue-eyed, little rosy-cheeked kids. But what made it funny was that they all actually looked like her mom's side of the family, not her dad's. So, in reality, they looked like Haans.

"I just thought Tess would command more influence." Amanda leaned her head back on the seat back and looked at him.

"It's possible the baby will have her eyes one day. I know Math really likes Tess's eyes," Hue stated.

"My brother really likes Tess's everything. But I think we both know for a fact he doesn't spend all his time looking at her eyes." Amanda grinned. Her brother had a fondness for his girlfriend's boobs, even when he had hated her. "I am so glad it all worked out for them."

"Me too. I like her more than Karen," Hue admitted.

Even if she knew that Krystal and Karen had been close through the years, it seemed the husbands weren't so fond of the wives.

Rolling her eyes at her ex-sister-in-law's name, Amanda was glad her brother was finally rid of her, even though they would forever be together through their three kids. Now she had a sister-in-law she loved … once they got married.

"Did you see the game on Sunday?" he asked, changing the subject to football. One of his favorites.

Amanda had finished her supper and was looking out at the snow falling. There wasn't enough to make driving dangerous, but it was coming down faster than when they had come to town. Shaking her head, she said, "No, I had book club."

"Of course. You can't miss book club." He teased her. Every other week, when he asked if she was watching the game that weekend, she had book club.

"No, I can't, it's the best part of my week. The week it happens, that is." She leaned her head against the back of the seat again.

"But it's the Vikings," Hue said of the team they all followed. Since Minnesota was only a few miles from Landstad, they claimed them as their own.

"But it's *book club*," she said in the same disbelieving voice he had used.

"Does anyone even read anymore?" He crumpled the paper that had been around his burger and threw it at her head.

She blocked it with her hand and missed, so it hit her head

anyway. "Yes, I read. The entire book club reads. Only you cannot read, Hubert." She loved calling him by his given name. He hated it.

"I can read; I just choose not to. What book are you reading this week?" He grabbed the crumpled wrapper from her lap and threw it at her again, only this time she didn't even try to block it, and it hit her in the face. Her sports skills were mediocre at best. She only watched sports.

"Fifty Shades of Grey." It was the go-to answer from the book club. It kept the old ladies out. But in reality, they all read different books, all about the same serial killer. Then they discussed it, recorded it, and released it to the internet as a podcast. Amanda had never listened to it, but Natalie Beckett, who took care of that end, said others did. Apparently, they were popular.

"Haven't you already read that one?" Hue asked.

"Yes, but we are taking it chapter by chapter, not wanting to miss a thing." She grinned.

"Learning anything?" He wiggled an eyebrow at her.

"Would you like me to tell you or show you?" She closed her eyes, but images of Hue Strong naked and bound to her bed had her snapping her eyes open, blushing.

"Either way, Nordskov." He reached over and tapped her nose as he looked into her eyes.

Amanda hoped he didn't notice the blush. "Maybe when we're done with it. Wouldn't want to get it wrong." She looked away from him since his blue eyes were boring into her.

"How is the clinic going, Dr. Nordskov?" he asked, changing the topic completely.

"I'm not a doctor, and you know that," was her answer, realizing that she had made him uncomfortable. She was just his friend's big sister, one who shouldn't tease him about sex.

"Nurse practitioner Nordskov just doesn't have the same ring to it."

"It's going well. More people are coming to me than before. I'm starting to be busy most days now." She told the truth. When she had first opened the doors of the clinic, she only got a handful of patients.

It had worried her in the beginning. Now, after almost a year, she was mostly busy.

"I'm glad you're there. It's nice to have a not-doctor closer than over an hour away," Hue admitted, something she heard a lot.

"Some of the people I don't see are the ones I know. They're uncomfortable coming to me. But I can understand that." She gathered all the empty wrappers and fry containers and put them back in the bag. Even the ball Hue had thrown at her.

"I wouldn't want to see a lot of the people in this town naked," he teased her. It was a part of her job that he liked to talk about. Naked people.

"Am I in that category?" She held the bag to her, realizing she shouldn't have said that.

"You, Nordskov, are at the top of the willing-to-see-naked category," he said with a wink and a smile. A joke.

Sighing in relief, she frowned. "Thanks, I think."

"Would you want to see me naked?" he asked, touching her nose with his index finger.

"I will when I show you what I learned in Fifty Shades of Grey." She tested him, but really, she kind of wanted to see him naked. A lot.

"I look forward to it." He looked away from her and shifted in his seat.

Again, she realized she had made him uncomfortable. Sometimes they could tease about sexual stuff, but sometimes it made him uncomfortable. She understood—she was his friend's older sister and not exactly his type.

"How is your mom?" She moved the conversation away from sex.

"You would know better than me," he answered since his mom was one of her patients.

"Are you mad she sees me?" She replied, glancing over at him.

"No, it's fine. She just doesn't tell me what she sees you about," he said, no longer smiling.

Sighing, she told him the truth. "I can't tell you."

"I know. I wish she would."

"I can tell you it's nothing for you to worry about." Amanda closed her heavy eyelids.

"I still worry. I mean, she is my mom. I just think she should tell me."

Amanda heard but didn't respond as the busy morning and emotional afternoon caught up with her, and she let her mind drift. But sadly, it drifted to thoughts of Hue tied to her bed. Really nice thoughts.

CHAPTER 2

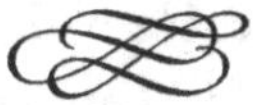

"And she is asleep," Hue said out loud to himself. Looking over at her, he smiled. She was a sleeper. Once things got a little boring, she was out. It probably had something to do with her nursing career. Being able to sleep when you could was ingrained into her.

It sounded funny to say he had slept with her many times. It was true, but it wasn't the sleeping people got excited to talk about. Every time she watched a sporting event on TV, she slept through most of it, and sometimes he would sleep during the game also. Right there, on the couch.

Since she had moved in across the hall from him just under a year ago, they would get together and watch games when neither had anywhere else to go or anything else to do. So, he had spent many hours cheering in silence so he wouldn't wake her up. Only to have her naturally wake up when there was five minutes left on the clock, so she could enjoy the last few minutes and claim she had watched the entire game—adamantly denying that she slept at all.

She always said she was a sports fan, but in reality, she only knew the players because she was able to retain information easily. Amanda had always been smart; smart enough she should have been the doctor he teased her about being. She had been the valedictorian and had breezed through college. After that, he had mostly lost touch with her as he had moved away for a dozen years, only to return to Landstad, hoping being back where he and Krystal had grown up would save what was left of their marriage. It had not, and she had gone back to Fargo and was married again. Happy again, with someone else.

But over the years, he had heard this and that about Amanda: married, divorced, great nurse. He had even seen her plenty over the years—Math's wedding, the kids' baptisms, birthdays, and some holidays. She had always made time for her family, and he had been lucky enough to have been invited to many of the family events.

Throughout those years, he had not spent much time with the adult Amanda, not until she moved in across from him. Before that, she had been there, but they hadn't spoken much. There had always been too many people around.

Now that they saw each other often, she was like an older sister who teased and taunted him. Then made sure he did the things he needed to, like family did. Except they weren't family, and she wasn't his sister. Because you aren't supposed to lust after your older sister.

With her asleep, he was able to look without her noticing. Her blonde hair was cut in a weird style that was long on top, but ended at her ears, and it was always styled nicely, even after a nap. Those blue eyes captivated him with their brightness.

Math had once told him that she thought she was short and fat, but she was only short compared to her sisters. And her curves made him want to run his hands over every one of them. He had always been into skinny girls until last year, when Amanda had moved in across from him. That was when everything changed.

His only issue with her was that she never saw him as more than anything but her brother's friend. No matter how many times he teased her about sex, she never caught on that he wanted it with her. She just took it as a joke.

Earlier today, he would have jumped at the chance to take her home. A long drive with them alone? Yes, please. But he knew that wasn't going to happen with her parents there since they would drive her home.

Until he saw the pain in her eyes in that hospital room. He didn't know how no one in her family saw it. It was as plain as her blue eyes that she was in agony. If it had been needed, he would have carried her out of the hospital. Instead, he had pushed her until she almost fell over in his rush to get her out of there.

In reality, he wanted out just as bad. It had bothered him to see his friend with another baby. It always bothered him to see others with a kid. He had wanted one for so long and had nothing to show for it. Never would.

Steadying her had been the easy part; letting her go had been twice as hard. He had wanted to pull her closer, to give her a hug to take away her pain. Take away the pain he was feeling. Instead, he had let her go, grabbing her hand as a consolation prize and holding on to it.

Once she had told him why the baby had bothered her so much, he completely understood. Who wouldn't feel emotional pain from that? But what had bothered him was that she had been around babies all the time. A year ago, she worked in the very same hospital they had just left, in the OB department. Why was it bothering her now suddenly and so much?

Reaching over, he lightly ran his hand over her smooth hair so as not to wake her. It never had before, so it wouldn't today either. It hadn't taken long in the pickup for her to get past the pain and turn back into the Amanda he knew. Once he had her laughing, he knew she was feeling better.

As they crossed the county line, Amanda started to stir. Must be the five-minute mark. Sitting up, she blinked a few times and looked around. "Where are we?"

"Right there is where I stopped you for speeding." He pointed to the exact spot.

Being a cop in a small town was mostly boring, until a lead-footed nurse practitioner flew past him. Then the nights got better. A lot more exciting.

"Which time?" She looked to where he was pointing. Only Amanda would admit that she had a lead foot. He had written the tickets that proved it.

"I think around four months ago?" He couldn't remember the exact date.

"Four and a half," she responded more to herself than to him since she said it so quietly.

Nodding at her answer, he said, "Could be. How many have I given you on this stretch?"

"No more than three," she said and then looked at him. "Possibly four."

"I should get your license taken away," he said, just wanting to rile her up a bit.

"Don't you dare, Hue. I have been good for a long time."

"You're right. I haven't seen that little gray, nondescript roadster speed through these parts lately." It wasn't like he had been looking, but he had been looking. There had only been four tickets, but far more warnings than anyone deserved.

"It's a Buick … they are not roadsters," she argued.

He loved that her chest heaved when she got riled up. "They are with your little foot on the pedals." He winked at her.

"I don't have little feet." Which was a lie; he had seen those feet many times over the years.

Picking up her hand, he took a minute to analyze it. "Little hands, little feet."

"That's only for guys, big hands, big … you know." She blushed as she said the end, or didn't say it, in this case.

"I don't understand what you're talking about." He was still holding her hand, unable to let go.

"I will tell you in my book report." She pulled her hand free as he stopped in front of their building.

"Me and my big hands look forward to it."

She opened her door and jumped out. She didn't acknowledge what he said, and he wondered if she heard him at all. Probably not.

At a slower pace, he got out of his pickup and followed her up the stairs to the second floor, above her clinic. She was already in her apartment when he got to the top of the stairs. Glancing at door two, he wondered if she would be up for watching something on TV. Maybe he would change and see if she wanted company. He wanted to spend more time with her.

CHAPTER 3

FINALLY, she could crawl into bed and hide under her covers like she had wanted to since she had gotten the call just after lunch that Tess had given birth. She had known Tess was in labor since the 4:00 a.m. call from Math. And it had been no surprise since she had been admitted the moment she got to the hospital. So, in reality, Amanda had figured she had more time, even just a few more hours. But it still wouldn't have been long enough. Days wouldn't have been long enough.

With a groan, she climbed out of bed and took off her tight pants that didn't seem too tight that morning. *Last day for those*, she decided and threw them on the closet floor. Her pile of clothes that didn't fit was growing. Of course, that meant there was a limited selection of ones that did. Deciding to take off her shirt, she threw that in the same pile. People must be thinking she was gaining weight at an astonishing rate, and she was.

As the weeks had worn on, she had started to eat better because she would lose the baby any day, and she wanted to take care of it for as long as she had it. The burger tonight had been crazy good, but crazy greasy and fatty. She had been fighting cravings for months now and had won most of the time, but today a burger was all she needed to be happy. A burger and Hue.

Climbing back into bed, she snuggled deep into the covers as she thought about Hue in his tight jeans and gray shirt. She would definitely love to give him step-by-step instructions on the actions in the steamy book. Though her book club was not reading the book and never would, she had read it and remembered enough of it to make Hue's toes curl. And hers too.

Flopping on her back, she couldn't believe that she had forgotten that Hue had given her a ticket. She had been coming home from Grand Forks and was speeding to get back since it was after midnight, and she had to work the next day. It was the last time she had slept with Paul before breaking it off with him again the next week. But it was that time that she had conceived the baby she was now carrying. It had basically been breakup sex since she knew it was over when they were together. It just took her a week to gather the courage to tell him. It wasn't the first time they had broken up, just the last time.

The disastrous relationship, if you can even call it that, had been on and off for three years. Mostly on, even though she hated that she was weak enough to be the other woman. And he was never going to leave his wife of twenty years. But she stayed because she thought that he loved her. In reality, what he loved was having someone who would come to him when he wanted sex. It wasn't her who was special.

Before she had taken the position in Landstad, she had miscarried his child, and he had accused her of trying to trap him. He had been all too happy when her so-called trap hadn't worked. It hurt even worse because he knew her medical history, and he knew she would lose the baby. But after moving here, he had called and called until she went back. Month after month, until she finally ended it in mid-June. At that point, she had finally had enough.

This time, there had been a parting gift. It wasn't until late August when she realized something wasn't right. After taking a home test, she was heartbroken she would have to go through it again. Since that day, she had waited for the inevitable end to this pregnancy. But this one had seemed more stubborn, and at twenty weeks, she was still carrying it.

So far, she had not seen a doctor about it. What could they do that they hadn't done before? There was no way to stop any of her other miscarriages. This one would be no different.

Except by next week, the pregnancy would be viable. This was one of her specialties, premature births, back when she was an OB nurse in the NICU. Next week, everything would change. If she could make it that long.

Turning her mind away from her sad future, she thought about her sexy neighbor and his big hands. He had held her hand twice today. While he held hers in the pickup, she felt liquid heat rush through her body. Her sudden interest in Hue Strong was definitely due to pregnancy hormones.

Sure, she had thought he was a nice-looking man over the years, even in high school when she had tutored him. She had daydreamed of him kissing her, but that had been a nerd's dream of having a football player. Now it was the nurse's dream of having the cop like her. In the end, it was just a fantasy.

Because to Hue, she was and would always be boring old Amanda Nordskov. He put up with her because he was friends with her brother. He treated her no different than he treated her other sisters.

Rolling over, she hoped her nurse's fantasy would follow her into sleep. Because her dreams had become way more erotic as her pregnancy went on. One of the only positives.

IT HAD BEEN five days since Hue had driven Amanda home from the hospital. Five days since he had talked to her. He had seen her around town and in passing a few times, but he hadn't been able to spend time with her. It was time to change that.

Today was Sunday, and he talked to Math, who said there would be no watching football for the new father. He also mentioned in passing that Mandy wasn't going out to see the baby today, which meant she was most likely in her apartment. And that was across the hall from him.

Grabbing a beer and a few bags of chips, he headed to her apartment. At his door, he looked at the chip selection, took out the ranch-flavored chips, and tossed them on the table by the door. Those were not welcome in her apartment. Not since the first time he had gone over there for football season in September.

They had been watching baseball for months, but football was different. So much better. At that time, she usually provided snacks, and he provided beverages. On that particular day, she was out of chips, which was a crime in itself, so he had volunteered to grab what he had from across the hallway.

Back in her apartment, he had tossed the bags between them so she could inspect them. Pulling the bag of the ranch chips out, she said, "You can't eat these here. Just the smell of them is making me sick."

At her words, he took the bag from her and opened it, making the smell fill the room. He looked at her to make some smart comment, but she had gone completely pale and already had slammed her hand to her mouth. She had barely made it to the bathroom before she was sick. Apologizing by bringing her a glass of water, he then tossed the chips in the hallway, not wanting to leave her. The instant sickness the chips had caused made him never bring them back.

Without knocking, he walked into her apartment. If she didn't want him there, she would have locked the door. It was Sunday, after all. The surprised look on her face as she watched him walk into her apartment as she sat at her table eating a sandwich made him chuckle.

"Ever knock, Hue?" She frowned cutely.

"Door's open, Nordskov. That means come in." He tossed the chip bags on the table.

"That's at my mom's house. And her driveway is a mile long, so she knows you are coming before you barge into her house." Her words sounded distracted by the end as she looked through the chip selection with interest. Might be the reason he always brought at least four kinds. As far as he could tell, she always picked a different kind—never the same old chips for Mandy.

"A Nordskov house is a Nordskov house." He put the beer in the fridge. Looking at what she had in there, he pulled out a bottle of water. "Fancy water, Nordskov? Are you getting snooty on me?"

"I need to drink more water, and you do too." She had opened a bag of chips and added some to her plate.

"Is that from my friend or my doctor?" He sat across from her. She was wearing her glasses today. Usually, she wore contacts, but some days she didn't bother with them. They made her look smarter and hotter.

"I am not a doctor. And I have never seen you in my office." She grinned.

"That's because I don't want to stand in front of you naked in your sterile clinic." He opened his beer.

"I don't make people just strip naked, Hue." She pointed a chip at him as she spoke, ate the chip, then added, "They always are offered a gown,"

"I am not taking my chances." He swiped her half-eaten sandwich and took a bite—turkey and cheese—then put it back on her plate. She glared at him for that move. "Have you seen the baby?"

She picked up the sandwich he had just bitten into and went back to eating it. "Yes, good baby check-up on Friday. She is doing great. No issues."

"Did you hold her?" he asked.

"Yes, it's my job. I'm fine, Hue. It was just that day. It was too much." He didn't believe her for a moment.

"If you're so okay, why didn't you go out there today to see the baby? Or yesterday?" He took a chip off her plate and ate it.

"I worked half a day yesterday, and today I need some me time." She pulled her plate a little closer to her, or a little further from him.

"I'm here," he pointed out.

"I didn't invite you." She again pointed a new chip at him and ate it.

"Your door was unlocked," he reminded her, pointing to it behind him.

"I didn't realize you had free access to my place when unlocked. I will have to make a point of locking it at night, so I don't end up with you in my bed." She took a bite of her sandwich, but her cheeks turned crimson at her words.

If only that was all it took. He would love to just climb into her bed one night. Any night. Sadly, he would do it every night if he had the chance. "Is that an invitation, Nordskov?" He winked at her.

With a roll of her eyes, she got up and took her now empty plate to the kitchen and put it in the sink. Today she was wearing Christmas green leggings and some kind of white sweater that was long enough to cover her butt from view.

Since she was not going to answer his question, he grabbed the chips to bring them to the living room. "You will need to change, lady."

She looked down at her outfit. "What? Why?"

"We can't have you wearing Packer colors. The home team will think you're not on our side." He looked down at her outfit.

"I think the home team will be okay. I don't want to change." She walked to the couch.

"You underestimate the home team. I know you have purple somewhere in this house." He put up his hands to block her from being able to sit down on the couch.

"Really? How many times have you seen me wear purple?" She threw up her hands.

"Nothing?" he questioned.

"No, I'm not that much of a fan." Her eyes went to the jersey he was wearing, and yes, he was that big of a fan.

"No wonder we never win the Super Bowl, Nordskov."

She laughed at his response. "You're blaming that on me?"

"Well, it isn't the players' fault."

"Blame me then. Can we just watch the game?" She turned the TV on and finally plopped onto the couch.

"I need you to at least lose the pants." He stood above her.

"No." She looked at him over her glasses. "The pants stay."

"Please," he said in a whiny voice.

"Can I at least put on another pair of pants, or do you need me just in my panties?" She folded her arms.

"Panties are preferable, but if you *neeeed* pants." His mind went straight to her sitting in nothing but panties, and his mind lost the shirt too. And suddenly, he lost interest in the game. He would prefer to spend hours watching her naked.

Getting up, she said, "I *neeeeed* pants."

Walking toward her room, he pulled off his jersey and said, "Hey, put this on. The home team will work harder for you then."

Tossing it to her, she almost caught it, but it slipped to the floor right at her feet. Picking it up with two fingers, she asked, "Have you washed this this year?"

"Of course, Nordskov. Right before the first game. It's only lucky if it's dirty."

"You're trusting me with your lucky shirt?" Her eyebrow went up in question.

"I trust you with everything." He watched her walk into her bedroom to change.

While she was gone, he went back to his place and grabbed another jersey from his closet. He was glad he had more than one, so he could share with her. Slipping it on, he hurried back to her apartment before she came out.

He was back on the couch when she came out in black leggings and the jersey that was a few sizes too big. She held out her arms so he could see she was wearing it, as if he wouldn't be able to see if she hadn't done the motion.

"Wait, you have another one? Now we look like the bench. Which of us are they going to call up first?" She was smiling as she sat down next to him.

"A true fan has a backup for a friend."

On the TV, the game had already started, and they had missed a few minutes, but he would rather see her in his shirt than watch any football game. Leaning back, he put his feet on the coffee table and watched the game for a while.

Amanda was beside him, but she wasn't watching the game. She was texting someone. Or maybe someone's. As her conversation continued, she turned and leaned against the side of the couch, not even pretending to watch the game. Every now and then, she chuckled at her phone.

Pulling the blanket off the back of the couch, he arranged it over the two of them. Then he took her feet that were almost touching his leg and put them on his lap. To his surprise, she didn't protest, just snuggled deeper into the blanket as he held on to her feet—her little feet.

Mindlessly, he watched the football game and rubbed her feet. She didn't protest, so he kept doing it. Soon, she put her phone down and looked over at the TV for a few minutes. The next time he looked at her, she was sound asleep.

He continued to hold her feet but had stopped rubbing them since he didn't want to wake her. When he was sure she was in a deep sleep, he reached over and pulled her glasses off, and put them on the coffee table.

Usually, she fell asleep in an uncomfortable position, waking up now and again during the game to readjusted, but today she slept right through. In fact, she slept until the game was over. He had thought about waking her before he left, but if she was sleeping, then she needed the sleep. Slipping out from under her legs, he regretted leaving. He tucked the blanket more around her shoulders and kissed her forehead lightly so as not to wake her up.

Closing the door as he left, he smiled. He loved Sunday football with her. Even when she slept through almost all of it. Or maybe it was that he enjoyed spending time with her, and football was just an excuse.

CHAPTER 5

Another Tuesday. She had made it to another Tuesday. Another week. Twenty-one now. The wait continued. She was now well into her second trimester, and she was tired all the time. Some days she would just go home from work, eat supper, and sleep until morning. On Sunday, she had slept from whatever time she fell asleep during the game until after eight. Hue had been long gone when she woke up.

Hue, one of her best friends, the guy she had known all her life. Or was it Hue, the star of all her X-rated dreams? Since she had been sleeping more, she had been dreaming more. Not that he hadn't been the star of them before the second trimester started or even since she moved back. But they had turned hotter over the past few weeks. Hormones.

She hadn't seen him since Sunday and didn't really know what she would say when she did see him. *Sorry, I fell asleep and didn't wake up for hours?* Seemed lame. Best not to say anything.

The bell above the door sounded, and her friend Ruth Kennedy walked in. Smiling at the woman she had known since forever, but had only become friends with recently, Amanda got up from her desk.

So far, she had not had time to hire a receptionist. Not that they would have a lot to do, but it would take some of the load off her. So far, the budget didn't stretch that far, so Amanda did everything in the office. Which meant she knew Ruth didn't have an appointment today.

"Ruth, how are you today?" It was an odd question, given that her friend had just walked into a health clinic, but sometimes she also just came to visit when things were quiet. Their offices were across the street from each other.

"Good, Mandy. How are you?" Ruth was her sister Kit's age, around thirty, and had lived in town her entire life. Currently, she was dating her former boss, an insurance agent named Anderson Miles. Amanda knew her well because she was in the book club with her.

"I'm good. It's getting cold out." Weather, always a safe topic.

"Yes. Time to get your winter stuff out," Amanda said.

"Seems like I just put it away," Ruth admitted nervously.

They both laughed. Winter was long in North Dakota, and everybody knew it. "Are you here for a social visit or more?"

Ruth smiled and said, "More."

"Why don't you come back, and we can talk?" Amanda was glad her calendar was empty and got up to lead Ruth down the hallway to the only exam room.

In the little room, both women sat in the chairs there. Amanda almost laughed at the memory of Hue insinuating that everyone got naked when they came to visit her. Here was Ruth, all fully dressed.

Ruth was the first to say something. "I am late."

Amanda saw that coming from a mile away. That was what it was like in a small town—you knew everybody's business. And on top of that, she knew the couple. And at book club the week before, Ruth had changed to wine instead of her usual mixed drinks. Amanda knew this was coming. Secretly, she was glad her friend had come to her to get it confirmed; some people had a hard time seeing someone they knew personally.

"Congratulations, Ruth." She jumped from her chair and gave her friend a hug, trying to be truly happy for her friend.

"Thanks, Mandy. I don't know what to feel. I want to confirm it before I say one way or the other." Ruth hugged her back and then sat down again.

"How does Anderson feel?"

"He's thrilled, but he is not the one who has to carry a baby. Or the one who has to tell my mother I am not married but having a baby." Ruth was wringing her hands.

"How about if you carry the baby and have him tell your mother? He deserves the wrath of the dragon." Amanda chuckled at the nickname Ruth's mother had received from Ruth's circle of friends in high school. It was still what many people called the woman, but it was a well-deserved name. "Let's make sure there is something to tell, then move on to who will do what."

It took less than an hour for Amanda to confirm that Ruth was right. With the verification, Ruth was able to show her excitement a little bit more. Amanda was happy for her friend, as happy as she could be on a Tuesday.

"I didn't think you would have the next baby in book club." Amanda logged information into her computer.

Ruth turned to her. "Who did you think?"

Laughing, she said, "I was thinking Hazel."

Their fellow book club member had just been married the previous month in a whirlwind marriage to a local preacher. Hazel was actually a lot younger than both Ruth and Amanda, and at twenty-four, she already had a son from a previous relationship. So, adding another seemed to be where Amanda had placed her bet. She had known Ruth wanted the ring before the baby. But then again, you couldn't always control when you got pregnant. She should know.

"Maybe she'll be next." Ruth smiled a little grin.

"Maybe. So, do you know how far along you are?" Amanda asked as she updated her file.

"Around seven weeks, I think. Maybe eight."

"Let's put it at seven. We can adjust if we need to." Amanda typed in the information.

"When do I have to see you again?" Ruth asked.

"I have to tell you that I can do all the appointments and things, but I cannot be involved in the birth. That's how it is. So, if you want to see someone else who can do everything, I understand. You'll have to go to someone new right when you maybe want a familiar face." Amanda set down her pen.

"No, I want you. You can pick who I deliver with. I think you know all the baby doctors around." Ruth smiled, because everyone knew she had worked in labor and delivery before. Small towns.

"Thank you, Ruth. So, I'll see you back in a month." Opening the appointment book on the computer, she went to a month from today, Tuesday. Another damn Tuesday.

"Do you want to do Tuesday again? It is exactly a month then, or move it?" she asked, almost tripping up on the word Tuesday. *It was only a day of the week, Amanda, and it happened every week.*

"No, that works for me. First thing in the morning, is that open?" Ruth asked.

She typed her name into the calendar as she bit her lip because it was starting to quiver. In a month, Tuesday won't matter anymore. "Yes, you can bring Anderson if you want."

"I will. A month on Tuesday." Ruth looked at her in confusion.

Fighting back the tears, she pretended to do more on the computer, but everything on the screen screamed *Tuesday*. Fighting back the despair, she said, "Yes. Can you show yourself out, Ruth? I've got to get the room cleaned up."

"Sure. Thanks, Mandy. I love having the clinic in town and that you're running it." Ruth gave her another happy hug. Or half happy. Because as much as she wanted to be happy for her friend, she wasn't able to.

Amanda remained seated as she watched Ruth leave and shut the door behind her. With the click, she broke down as the sobs overtook her. Tuesday. She would see Ruth every Tuesday and see her baby grow. Every Tuesday, even after her own baby was long gone. How was she going to be happy for her friends when their happiness at being pregnant and having babies was killing her inside?

The day that Ruth was scheduled to come in, Amanda would be on her twenty-fifth week. But how many weeks would she have been without it by that time? Two? Three? Why can't it just happen so she can get back to her life? The constant threat was causing her more stress than anything she had ever faced in her professional career.

Breathing deeply to control her emotions, she chanted to herself, "Enjoy the time you have with the baby, enjoy the time you have with the baby." Because it was the only time she would have with the baby she wanted so bad, and it hurt to think about what was going to happen soon. Too soon.

CHAPTER 6

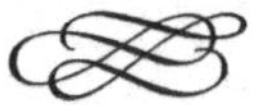

"I THOUGHT that we decided the team needs you to wear a jersey," Hue was saying as he looked her up and down on Sunday afternoon. It had been a week since he had given it to her, and she had worn it almost every evening after work. As of Thursday, sadly, it no longer smelled like him, which wasn't why she was giving it back. Once the smell had gone, she had lost interest in wearing it.

"I have to give that back to you." She hadn't washed it since she didn't know the rules on lucky shirts.

"No, you keep it, but you have to wear it." He was looking again at her Orange Landstad Tigers sweatshirt over the black leggings. They were the only type of pants she owned that fit her anymore. He, of course, was in basketball shorts and a Vikings jersey. His legs were mouthwateringly muscly.

"It's book club, Hue. I'm not wearing a football jersey to Ruth's."

"But you'll wear that?" He waved his hand over her outfit as if her outfit didn't measure up.

"I support the home team, but not your home team, apparently." They had both been Landstad Tigers in high school, and she still supported the local team. He did too, but not on football Sundays.

"The Tigers aren't playing an important game today." He smiled.

"Nor is your team, just a regular game," she argued.

His hand slammed to his chest like he was really injured. "Take that back, Nordskov. All games are important. Each and every one brings us closer to playoffs."

At his stern face, she laughed and pushed past him to the couch. "It's just a game, Hubert."

He grabbed her from behind and lifted her off the floor so she couldn't reach it.

"Put me down."

"First, you have to say the game is important." His words came from right behind her ear and sent a shiver down her spine.

What was it about just his voice that could turn her on now? "Your game is important," she whispered, unable to catch her breath while he held her in his strong, warm arms. Her body was pressed into his, and all she could smell was him.

"Now say that you will never ever call me Hubert again." His hands moved, so he was almost touching her breast now.

If she just moved the right way, he would be. "But you call me Nordskov all the time," she argued and shifted slightly.

She felt him touch her ear with his mouth as he said, "Say it, Nordskov."

"Never," she breathed out. Her mind had them naked already, and she was getting turned on just thinking about it.

"Nordskov." He slid his hand up, and it grazed the underside of her breast.

"Hue," was all she could say as his mouth lightly touched her neck.

"Mandy," he whispered as he placed a few more kisses while she leaned her head to give him better access to her sensitive skin, wanting more. She wondered if it was just another dream—a vivid dream. One she never wanted to wake from.

Lowering her to the ground slowly, he trailed kisses across her neck. His hands skimmed her breasts. Instantly, she regretted wearing the comfortable, thick sweatshirt and wished she was naked. Wished they both were naked.

A vibration between their bodies made her jerk away. What was that? His arms left her body as he swore to himself, taking his phone from his pocket. Amanda knew it was the reason behind the vibration. The swearing must be because of his instant regret about what had happened between them.

Running his hand through his hair, he answered the phone. "Math?"

She turned and watched him listen to her brother. He wasn't looking at her, and when he did, he turned away so that she couldn't hear what they were talking about.

Whatever just happened, he regretted it already. Sadly, he was not as affected by it as she had been, but then again, he didn't have pregnancy hormones coursing through his body. Nor did he have a sexy woman in his arms. He must have realized it was just Amanda.

Loudly she told him, "I'm going to book club. Just let yourself out." Slipping on her shoes, she headed out the door, down the stairs, across the street, and up Ruth's stairs. Yes, she was out of breath when she got to Ruth's door. Once again, she decided to start exercising. A short run shouldn't take that much out of her. Or maybe she was still out of breath from Hue touching her? Either way, she should start exercising.

She kicked her shoes off as she knocked on the door and went inside, calming herself as best she could. Ruth knew she was coming but still looked surprised she was there. It was book club. It didn't matter that she was half an hour early.

Ruth and Anderson were in the kitchen making snacks for the afternoon. Well, actually, Anderson was making snacks. Ruth was organizing the alcohol selection from a barstool, but mostly she watched him cook. Both looked her way as she walked into the apartment.

"Hi, guys." Ignoring their confused looks, she took off her coat, glad she wasn't outside very long since she could barely zip it anymore. And sadly, winter was only just beginning.

"Hi, Mandy, you're early." Ruth tapped the stool beside her.

"Yes, I didn't want to start watching the football game, so I came over. Hope you don't mind." She shouldn't have come over this early.

She didn't want to make small talk with these two. But Hue had been in her apartment, and where else would she have gone? Add to that she in no way wanted to talk to Hue right now.

Ruth shook her head. "No, you can come over whenever you want to. You can watch Anderson cook with me."

"I never get to watch Anderson cook." She looked at the man as she sat down.

"Now I'm going to get nervous and mess up." Anderson smiled at the two women, though he didn't really look at Amanda. He only had eyes for his girlfriend.

"Can I get you something to drink?" Ruth asked, pointing at the alcohol bottles already on the counter. Book club meant drinking, and the assortment of bottles showed just how much.

"Sorry, I'm on call again. But if you can make it look like I'm drinking, I won't get all the questions from everyone. I mean, if they know half of us aren't drinking, they might get self-conscious about it." It had been months of excuses about not drinking, too many months now.

Ruth nodded in agreement. "I guess. Just Coke then?"

"Yes, thanks. What are you doing tonight, Anderson?" Amanda turned her attention to Ruth's boyfriend, taking the conversation away from alcohol.

"Since our man numbers are getting up there, we're trying a poker night on book club night. I've invited Rafferty as an extra." Anderson worked with Rafferty Brooks at the insurance office. Rafferty was

another one of her sister Kit's former classmates. He was also in Ruth's, but everyone in town knew the two of them did not get along. Even if they both got along with Anderson.

"Sounds interesting. Is Ruston playing?" she asked in interest. Ruston had just married Hazel and was the preacher at Amanda's church, which meant he might not be one for gambling and card games.

"It's at his house," Anderson said with a wink.

"Do you have to make food for that, too?" Amanda asked as Ruth handed her the glass of pop.

"Yup, these are to-go, and those are for here." He pointed at the separate groups of snacks.

"We're lucky to have you, Anderson. Ruth would serve us burnt toast." Amanda looked at her friend.

"I would not," Ruth argued with a smile. "I would simply not make anything."

All three laughed at her answer. Ruth had spent most of her adult life avoiding cooking and had been successful in her endeavor.

"What is so funny?" Rafferty Brooks came into the house without knocking. He left his coat on but came over to the kitchen.

"Ruth's cooking skills," Anderson said as he closed the lids on containers with his to-go food.

"I can see the joke," Rafferty said, but he didn't laugh. Turning to her, he said, "Hey, Mandy."

Mandy had always enjoyed that Rafferty was a flirt. It felt nice to have him pay her attention. Knowing it would never go anywhere was what made it fun.

"Hi, Rafferty. I hear you've been invited to the poker game tonight."

Standing between Ruth and her, he reached for something Anderson had just packed. With a shift, he bumped her shoulder and turned to her. "Yup, I am an honorary book club widower."

"Congratulations," she said, waiting for the sexual need to rise in her that always happened when Hue was around. But it seemed the pregnancy hormones were not in it for Rafferty. How was it that Rafferty didn't have her senses on high alert like Hue? A man was a man, right?

But looking back, she had only gotten these over-sexualized thoughts with Hue, never with anyone else. Never the delivery guy or the guy at the post office or old friends that she saw on the street. Just Hue. It seemed her hormones were damn selective. In a good way, at least.

Not that it mattered, anyway. Hue was not into her. She was definitely not his type. His ex-wife was tall, brunette, and had been the homecoming queen.

The guys headed out, leaving the apartment quiet in their wake. "So, is Tess coming?" Amanda asked to fill the silence.

"Haven't you talked to her?" Ruth asked in confusion.

Amanda understood; she and Tess usually talked all the time. Being almost family had made them closer than if they were just friends. Except Tess was now busy with a baby. A baby Amanda longed to have. Except she was stuck waiting for the end of hers.

"No, sorry. I've been busy this week." Amanda knew the response was not really true, but she hoped Ruth didn't notice.

Ruth looked at her closely before stating, "She thinks you're avoiding her. Are you?"

"No, of course not," she argued, taking a drink from her pop.

Ruth looked in her eyes and held them for a moment. "Tess is coming, and you should make a point to talk to her."

"I will." Amanda looked away from Ruth's intense blue gaze.

She was relieved when Natalie and Hazel showed up at the same time, deep in a conversation that spread to Ruth as they entered the room. Soon, Amanda's cousin Mia bounced in from her apartment, which was the building next to Amanda's. Tess was running late, so Natalie started to set up for the recording as the group chatted.

Amanda moved from her stool to her usual spot at the table between Mia and Hazel. To her surprise, Hazel took the chair next to Natalie this week. Well, no surprise, since the two had been getting closer the last few weeks. The hatred that had once simmered between the two had fizzled since they had both found love over the last few months. Amanda was happy to see them getting along again, because they had been close to inseparable in high school just a half-dozen years ago.

Mia was chatting with Ruth across the table about some event she was supposed to be planning for Christmas. Ruth was making suggestions about advertising. Amanda's cousin was excited about what Ruth was suggesting. But Amanda wasn't paying attention, her mind was back in her apartment with Hue. Always back with Hue lately.

Looking at them all over her glass as she drank, she realized that she did not want to be here today. She wanted to go home again and wait. Normally, she loved these women and looked forward to these biweekly get-togethers to chat about a topic none of them talked about in their day-to-day lives. Serial killers. It was each one's secret obsession.

In January, her second month back in Landstad, Mia had been invited to a book club with Ruth and Tess, who had organized the event. Well, not an event, just a book club. They had met the next day at Mia's restaurant, and Mia had begged Amanda to go with. Both had usually read and shared the same books.

Reluctantly, Amanda had gone to the Sunday afternoon meeting, and it had started from there. It helped that Hazel and Natalie had both crashed the get-together also, so she wasn't the only one.

One of the first things the book club decided was that they would not read the same book, just the same topic. In their case, it was books about the same serial killer. Natalie, a librarian, was in charge of making sure that no two people read the same book. The way they did it was so that each came to the meeting with a different prospect, a different angle. It worked great and usually had them arguing about this and that.

What had started as an innocent book club about not innocent things had turned almost immediately into something different, nothing Amanda had ever even heard of: a podcast. Natalie had suggested it at their first meeting, and by the third, they were recording their conversations. Natalie did all the work and put it out on the internet. To everyone's surprise, people listened to them. They even waited for the next recording to come out.

They had purposefully never told anyone what book club really was. The only rule was that you couldn't tell unless you were married. So far, only Hazel should have been able to tell her husband, but Amanda suspected that the other men in her friend's lives knew. Since Tess had a baby with Amanda's brother, he must know. But he had never asked her about it or teased her about it, so maybe not.

Keeping it a secret had started the first day they met. Tess was the bank's president; Amanda worked at the clinic; Ruth, at that time, worked as a personal assistant downtown; Mia was a popular person in the community; Natalie worked at the public library; and Hazel was a single mom. None had wanted to be associated with serial killers. Now that they had fans, it might not be so bad, but they still all had to be professionals in this little town.

Natalie had all the equipment out, and the group was ready to go by the time Tess came into the apartment. She had never been late before, but it seemed having a new baby made the most punctual woman lose track of time. Or maybe it was Math, who hated being separated from his girlfriend, even for a few hours.

Smiling an apology, Tess set the baby carrier on the couch softly and walked away from it. The movements made Amanda realize that the baby was sleeping. Tess slid into the chair beside her and put on her headphones. Everyone glanced at the baby as Natalie tapped her nose—that meant silence—and started to record.

Hazel handed Tess the remaining pair of headphones as she sat down. Natalie insisted they wore them, something about sounds and echoing. But she was in charge, so they wore them.

By the time Amanda pulled off her headphones, the group had all but solved the West Mesa Bone Collector mystery. Unfortunately, there were three different theories on who did it, and nobody was willing to budge on their theory. So maybe not *completely* solved in one afternoon.

Amanda was feeling so much better and was happy she had come. Not that she had ever missed one of their get-togethers. For the last couple, she had forced herself to show up and always felt better when she left.

Tess's baby had slept through the entire thing, including a very vocal fight between Natalie and Mia that had the rest watching the baby for even a hint she was awake. But it seemed that when Natalie had stopped recording, the baby remembered that her job was to cry and eat.

When Tess had her settled in her arms, the group was completely focused on the baby. Asking all the questions that new mothers get. Tess answered them with just a touch of humor she always brought.

Amanda had always liked Tess, even when her idiot brother didn't think he did. And she hated that she had let the baby come between them. Hated that she was so consumed by emotions, she couldn't seem to control this time.

"So, have you named her yet?" Natalie asked. At this point, after almost two weeks, the couple had not agreed on a name. Both were too stubborn to let the other have their way. It was a lot like their relationship, but it worked for them. In the end, at least, since the middle was always a bit bumpy.

"No, not yet. I want Elizabeth, Ellie. Cute." Tess handed the baby to Ruth, who cooed at her.

"What does Math want?" Ruth asked, still looking at the baby.

"Mathias wants Terezilya. I just don't want to name her after me," Tess confided.

The name rolled off Tess's tongue. It was the only indication that Tess was born and spent her younger years in Russia. Her family emigrated to the states when she was already school age.

"But it's your mom's name. Tradition." Amanda was well aware of the argument her brother had about the name. A name that was not only Tess's mother's but her own name as well.

"But there are so many others in my family who carry that name." Tess came from a huge family who liked to use the same names over and over.

"What nicknames could you use?" Hazel asked, taking the baby from Ruth before Ruth was ready to hand her off.

"They have all been used. All of them," Tess insisted.

"How about the middle name?" Hazel looked at the baby, and Amanda met Ruth's eyes and winked. Ruth took a drink of her wine to cover her laugh.

"Same issue. Alexandrina, after my father, and every first-born grandson or granddaughter. Overused," Tess explained.

"Then go with Elizabeth. Damn tradition. Start a new one with Betsey," Mia said. She was a bit tipsy.

"Tell that to Mathias," Tess told her, then frowned. "Not Betsey, though."

"Give me your phone. I will text him." Mia waved her hand at her friend. Everyone knew she would do it.

"I don't think I want you drunk-texting my man, Mia," Tess said and laughed. What made it funny was that Mia and Math were cousins.

Natalie had gotten her turn but had handed the baby off quickly to Mia. Mia, of course, was maybe too tipsy for the baby. Amanda took the bundle from her cousin before Mia forgot she was holding the baby.

The baby was light in her abundance of pink blankets, and the smell of baby wafted over her. Amanda felt behind the baby's neck. Temperature was fine. Opening the blanket a little, she saw the baby was in a pink sleeper with a sheep on it. She had her fingers over the baby's chest, heartbeat was good. Then she ran her hand over the downy white hair on her head. Soft spot was good. She was as healthy as an almost two-week-old baby could be.

As she was looking at her little face, the infant's blue eyes popped open and stared at her. Of course, the baby couldn't see her—her sight was still poor at this age. When the baby gave her a lopsided grin, it was obviously just gas. Amanda said to the baby quietly, "Zia."

Turning to her future sister-in-law, if her brother would get his act together, she asked, "Are there any Zia's?"

Handing the baby back to Tess, the mother looked at the infant closely. "No, I never thought of it. Nobody else has, either. I will talk to Mathias. Zia Nordskov."

"And Amanda names another baby." Mia lifted her glass for a toast but was completely ignored. "How many is that, Mandy?"

"Leave Mandy alone, Mia," Ruth chastised Mia with a hard look. "I have an announcement."

Amanda leaned back in her chair, just happy she knew beforehand and had been able to steel herself for what was going to be said. Not even listening, she let the others congratulate their friend.

Hugs went around and questions for the soon-to-be Mom.

Tess turned to her and quietly said, "You don't seem too excited for Ruth."

Amanda turned and replied, "I am. I'm just letting the others get excited. She is my patient."

"Oh, it just seemed like you were being distant. Again," Tess stated.

"I'm sorry I've seemed distant. I've had a lot on my mind lately." She admitted some of the truth.

Tess seemed satisfied with the answer and let it drop. Soon everyone was leaving, and Amanda walked with Mia across the street. How fun it had been earlier in the year when there had been four that lived downtown. Ruth, Mia, Amanda, and Tess had all been within a block of each other. Now Tess was living at the farm with Mathias, and Ruth was probably going to find something bigger with the baby coming. A short era was coming to an end.

With a goodbye, they separated, and Amanda walked slowly to her place, making sure her younger cousin made it inside. Once Mia's door was closed, her pace increased. It was getting cold out at night, so she didn't linger.

Happily, she let herself into her apartment and, for some reason, she had thought Hue might still be there. But he had been gone for hours. It was only 7:00 p.m., but Amanda knew her day was over. She was exhausted.

Before she could rethink her decision, she took the jersey Hue had given her and left it on the hanger she kept it on, took it across the hall, and hung it on his door handle. She shouldn't keep the shirt; it was his. She wasn't even a big sports fan. In the beginning, she had watched to bond with her dad and brother, but now she watched because it was relaxing. Something that took her mind off everything around her. Except Hue. It made her think a lot about Hue.

Shedding her clothes, she climbed into bed and snuggled into the cold blankets, waiting for them to warm up. She would miss his shirt —she really did like to wear it, and it smelled like him. Fresh air and outdoors. Hue. It was also a shirt she could fit into. Those were lacking in her closet these days, but she wouldn't complain. She would never complain as long as her baby was still growing.

CHAPTER 7

HUE WAS NEVER GOING to forgive his best friend for as long as he lived. Math had finally come between him and a woman. It hadn't happened in all the years they went through school together, and the female population in their class hovered at just around twelve. And not when they were both carefree, divorced men about town at the same time. But today, he had come between him and Amanda.

Not literally, but when he had called, he had destroyed a moment Hue had wanted for so long. She had been in his arms. And she was responding to his touch. He was almost sure she moaned!

Grabbing her and teasing her about her loyalty to his team had been a game they played over the past year. But when she had laughed as she pushed past him, he just grabbed her, holding her so that she couldn't touch the ground and taunting her until she gave in.

It had backfired the moment his body felt hers pressing against him, her perfume surrounding him. When he had accidentally almost touched her breast, the moment turned, and all he wanted to do was kiss her. And when he did, she had given him permission by moving her head to allow him to touch her, kiss her.

Then Math had called, and she was out of his arms before he knew what was happening. Math, who was just bored and calling about the game being played. A game nobody even cared about. He and Amanda hadn't even turned the TV on yet. So, he let his friend rattle on about the game and tried to sound like he had been watching. Not kissing the neck of his older sister and loving the smell of her perfume.

Hearing her say she was leaving made him turn and watch her go. But with Math on the phone, he couldn't stop her. What was he going to say to his friend, *sorry, Math I have to go. I want to smell your sister's perfume again, maybe kiss her lips this time?* That would have gone over well.

Oddly, he knew Math wouldn't be upset if Hue ever dated any of his sisters. Or maybe Mandy would be different. The entire family was a little more protective of Amanda than the other two sisters. He had noticed it over the past year at family events. Maybe it had been going on for longer, but he hadn't been around to see it.

After she had left him alone in her apartment, it had felt weird not having her there with him. He hurried over the window and was able to watch her walk across the street to Ruth Kennedy's place above the rental office. From his vantage point, he watched her blonde head enter the stairway to her friend's upstairs apartment.

At the end of the call, Math asked if he wanted to go to a poker game. He looked at the apartment Amanda was in all afternoon and evening and said sure. So, within a few minutes, Math had picked him up, and they drove together to Ruston Abbot's house.

"What is this?" Hue asked his friend in confusion. The man was a preacher, after all. Could they even have poker night at his place? Weren't there laws about that?

"Poker night with the book club widowers. This is our first time," Math explained.

"Pastor Abbot's house?" Hue knew of the man, but not the man himself. Hue attended a different church in town when he attended at all.

"Yup, he was the one who came up with the idea. If it works out, we might have to change poker to something else." Math parked the pickup.

With nothing better to do, Hue got out of the truck and followed his friend into his preacher's house to play cards. Having never been in Ruston's house, he was surprised to see how homey it was, but the place had a woman's touch now that he had married Hazel.

They had been the last to arrive, with Anderson Miles, Rafferty Brooks, and Sam Sullivan already there. He knew them all, but he didn't know any of them well. As the beers were passed around, the men talked about book club. They discussed the book of the week, which was not what Amanda had said it was. In truth, it was a book about a serial killer. Remembering how she had promised a book report on the book she was reading, he wondered if she would tie him up for sex or to murder him? He hoped the former.

Very little poker was played, but many stories were told about the women meeting across town. He learned that they always met at Ruth's place, always drank, and always argued. Also, that it had only been going on since last January.

Sadly, he didn't learn anything interesting about Amanda, but he did learn a lot about the other five women, and he understood why she got along with them all. They had found friendship in a small town with people who were mostly different from them but somehow the same.

Just after 7:00 p.m., Hazel and Natalie came into the house, both a little tipsy and laughing as they walked in. As if on cue, everyone got up to leave. It seemed that when the men got their ladies back, they were done with their mens' night. He knew exactly how they felt—he wanted Amanda back, too. Back in his arms.

Math dropped him off and picked up Tess and the baby at the same time. Waving goodbye to the little family, he looked up at Amanda's window since he was on the opposite side of the street. Her lights were off. Was she already in her bedroom, a window he couldn't see? Or was she still at Ruth's?

At the top of the staircase, he saw the jersey hanging on his door. She must be home. Unlocking the door, he wondered what it meant that she had returned it. Would she not watch football with him anymore? Did she not want to be his friend anymore? Was she mad about the kiss?

Either way, he decided he was not excepting the jersey back. How could he? Every time he saw it, he would see her in it and how it bothered him that it covered her butt so he couldn't see it. And how much he wanted to just take the thing off her.

Taking it off his door handle, he took it over to hers, leaving it there. Would she accept that he wasn't being kicked out of her life? That next Sunday, he would be back to watch the game with her, whether she liked it or not.

* * *

By Saturday, he knew that seeing her on Sunday was completely out. Through Math, he had gathered that she would be going to church with her parents, then to her parents' house for lunch. After that, it was book club again, an odd week due to some of the members wanting to be out of town the following weekend, which was Thanksgiving.

This week had been a total miss for Hue in his Amanda sightings. None. Monday had been a long one for him at work, and on Tuesday, she hadn't made it home from the clinic until after eight. Or at least that's when he heard her door slam across the hall. Wednesday and Thursday, he was out at Math's to help him sort cattle in the evenings, and she had not shown up. Friday, he had actually spotted her at the café at lunchtime but hadn't been able to talk to her before she left.

Now it was Saturday evening, and her apartment was completely quiet. No TV running, no sounds of movement. Not that he was listening for her …

He was itching to cross the hallway and knock on the door to see if she was there, but he had no excuse for doing it. Nothing that wouldn't seem weird for him to be there. So, he just watched TV and thought about her.

Unable to control it any longer, he jumped up and went to her door and knocked. Waiting for her to answer, he tried to come up with an excuse, but none were coming to mind. Knocking again, he looked at his watch. It was 7:00 p.m., so she should be in there. Unless she was gone, like he had suspected all day.

One more knock had the door opening, and he was looking at her finally. After almost a week, there she was in front of him. He could tell she had been sleeping—her hair was a little messed, and she looked warm and just-woke-up sexy. "What do you want, Hue?" She was alert as always after a nap.

"Milk? I'm out and need a cup." Brilliant, lame excuse.

Her face said he was annoying her, and she didn't need to get up for this. "Fine, come on."

Leaving the door open as she went into her apartment, he followed. She was wearing an oversized Landstad Tiger's T-shirt and gray sweatpants. The outfit should not be sexy, but on her, it was. He wanted to pin her to the wall and see if she was wearing a bra under that shirt. He knew she wasn't.

He shoved his hands in his pockets because his dick was enjoying the idea of no bra way too much. No need for her to suspect how he felt about her or, more importantly, how he thought about her. Indecent thoughts he shouldn't be having about her at all. But he always was.

"Is the store closed?" she asked as she dug into the fridge for milk.

"Ah, no, just too cold to go out again tonight," he said; nothing else came to mind.

"It's gotten cold lately, hasn't it?" She shook her milk container and then looked into the carton. Right now, she wasn't wearing her glasses, and he suspected she wasn't wearing her contacts, either. For the first time, he wondered if she was far or nearsighted.

"I know, but I'm out of milk."

"I think there's enough in here." Shrugging, she handed him the carton.

"I don't want to take the last of your milk." He felt guilty suddenly. He actually had milk, and he didn't want her to be without for no real reason.

"I have another one." She pointed to the now closed fridge.

"What have you been up to today?" Not wanting to leave, he tried to keep her talking.

"Nothing really. I had to read my book for tomorrow and got caught up on paperwork."

"Sounds like you wasted a Saturday," he teased.

"What did you do that was so great?" she countered.

"I watched three football games." He watched her roll her eyes at him.

"Please, they were only college," she said, as if that was worth her time.

"You bet, sweetheart, but one day some of those players will be playing in the NFL in a game that you will sleep through, maybe even the super bowl." He grinned at her.

"I do not sleep during football. I rest my eyes." She argued the same argument she'd used a hundred times.

"For hours at a time?"

"My eyes are strained," she stated, as if it were a fact.

He took her chin in his hand and looked into her eyes. Her beautiful blue eyes. "They don't look strained to me."

She blinked at him and said, "I was just sleeping, so they have rested today."

Running his thumb across her jaw, he said, "I—" But his phone rang from his pocket.

He wanted to ignore it, but her eyes looked away from his in the direction of the ringing. She stepped away and turned back to the kitchen.

Sliding his phone out of his pocket with the hand that had just been touching her, he almost cursed when he saw Math's name on the screen. Again. Did the man have cameras set up in this apartment? Because he knew exactly when to call to break up anything Hue was trying to start with the man's sister.

"Math," he mumbled and looked at her. "I will see you later."

"Yeah, bye, Hue." She leaned against the counter as far from him as she could get.

Leaving the apartment, the phone was still ringing. Hue was still mad at his friend. But at his apartment door, he answered anyway. "Math."

"Hue, what are you doing?"

"Just watching a game," he lied. Sure, he had been watching a few minutes before, but his mind had been on Mandy, not football.

"Mom wanted me to tell you that you are invited to Thanksgiving at her house if you want to spend the day with a bunch of Nordskovs." Math sounded excited, just like when they were in high school.

He wanted to spend the day with only one Nordskov, and it wasn't the one he was talking to. But with the invitation, he would be in the same house as Amanda for a few hours.

"Sure, my mom is going to Jill's this year." His mom actually almost always went to his sister's for holidays. His sister had produced four kids, all girls, for her to spoil. Hue was invited every time also, but he usually passed to let his mom and sister have some time together.

"That's what Mom thought. Hey, did you hear that Mandy named the baby?" Math said.

"No." But he was very interested. Anything about the woman was interesting to Hue.

"Yup, she was holding her at book club and just said, 'Call her Zia.' It was perfect, and so is Mandy. All she had to do was look at the baby, and the perfect name came to her. So, Zia is named for her mom, just like I wanted. My sister came through for me," Math stated, as if Mandy had actually been on his side of the argument.

Hue was sure she was not.

"I doubt she came up with it just so you could win an argument with your not-wife." Hue threw in the last part because his friend should be marrying the woman. He knew Math had proposed countless times and had been shot down on every one of them.

"Don't start. We have talked about it, and we are not ready." Math said the same excuse the two always said. The excuse the woman was constantly giving him, because there was no 'we' in the reasoning. Math would have married her months ago.

"What are you waiting for? Another baby? She wants a ring." Hue chuckled.

"I'll get there. I need a ring and a perfect moment." What he needed was to wear her down. Tess Thorn was a stubborn woman, and Math had to put in the time to get her to be his wife.

"Any moment is perfect if she loves you," Hue told him in all seriousness.

"You're such the romantic, Hue." Math laughed with him, taking no offence.

"That I am," Hue mumbled.

"We have to find you a woman. Have you even dated since the divorce?" Math asked interestedly.

"No, but neither did you, and you got some chick knocked up," Hue deflected, wondering if Amanda had gone back to bed or if she had left her door unlocked so he could join her. He couldn't knock her up, but he would sure like to give it a try for a while.

His friend just laughed. "Not just some chick, that would have been easy. I had to knock up a stubborn chick."

"Who I am going to tell you called a chick on Thanksgiving." Hue laughed, knowing exactly how badly that would turn out for his friend.

"If you do, you will not get to be best man when I do marry her," Math threatened.

"I already was your best man; didn't seem to work. Maybe you should try someone else this time." Each had been best man at each other's failed first marriages.

"Nope, I'll take my chances. Because I am going to be there for your wedding one day."

"Never again. I am not going through that again." He was done with marriage and everything it entailed. Not even his sexy neighbor could change his mind about that.

"For the right lady, it is worth it," Math said dreamily.

"And you called me the romantic." Hue sat heavy on his couch.

"After Thanksgiving, I'm going to have Tess set you up with one of her friends." Hue held his breath. Amanda? She was one of Tess's single friends.

"Who?" He tried not to sound excited.

"I can't remember her name. She works at the bank. Tall and pretty. Just like you like them." He could see Math racking his brain for the name. Something Math wasn't very good with: remembering people.

"Maybe," he said noncommittally. That was his type until Amanda came to town. Now he was more into the shorter, pretty ones. Or just the one.

"Definitely going to do that," Math said before he hung up the phone.

Leaning back on the couch, he closed his eyes. He didn't want to date someone from the bank. All he wanted was to go back to before the phone call and kiss the woman across the hallway. Finally kiss her.

CHAPTER 8

Amanda checked her phone for the second time, and the Vikings were still not playing this Thanksgiving. But she wanted to wear the jersey again. Badly. She had worn it to work on Wednesday, and it had been comfortable, and it fit without her having to check the mirror all the time to see if she looked fat. And two of her patients had noticed and relaxed into talking about sports before telling her why they were there.

Looking down at the white sweater she was wearing, she knew it made her look fat, but everything did today. Because she was fat. Her middle was finally bigger than her hips, not really a great accomplishment. But an achievement just the same. The one plus side of getting fat was that her breasts no longer fit into her bra. They were huge. Sadly, nobody was enjoying them, though Amanda looked at them every once in a while.

Fat. Of course, she knew she wasn't fat. But when she miscarried the baby, she would be left with the fat the pregnancy had brought. So, calling it fat now would help her later.

Taking off the nice sweater, she slid on a Landstad Tigers sweatshirt—not so bad in the bulky sweatshirt. And it had a tummy pocket to put her phone in. Adding orange leggings to match, she decided she was ready. No effort this year for the holiday, it looked like. Her mom would comment.

It was close to 10:00 a.m. when she pulled into her parents' yard. Like every year, she had needed to get to the dinner early to help her mom. Walking into the house, it already smelled of the meal ahead. Following voices to the back of the house, she found her mom and two sisters already mixing ingredients.

"Hello," she said to everyone in the room.

"Mandy is here," Her little sister Kit said unnecessarily.

Everyone had turned to see her already.

"Mandy *is* here," Amanda emphasized the is.

"I thought you would be here a little later." Her mom, Dolly, rushed over to her and kissed her cheek. "I figured you and Hue would ride together since you live right there."

"I didn't know Hue was coming." Amanda had no idea. Actually, she had been hoping for a reprieve from her thoughts about whatever-happened the other night when she had thought he was going to kiss her. She could have sworn he was going to kiss her. But she knew better, she was Amanda.

"His mom went to Jill's again this year, so I had Math invite him," her mom said, rushing back to the pot she had been stirring.

"Well, that's good. Being alone on a holiday is awful," Amanda said, and her sisters agreed. But it had been exactly how she had wanted to spend this one. Alone.

"Mandy, Mom doesn't need us all. Come sit down," Kit said from the table she was sitting at.

Her sister was right, there were too many cooks in the kitchen, and it was hot in there already. Sitting by her sister, she asked, "How is it going?"

A year ago, they had been close, but now they barely spoke. Mostly because Amanda had moved away from the town they both had lived in. And partly because she wasn't talking to many people these days.

"Good." Her sister smiled a little too wide. It had been a long time since her sister had been good. Her first husband had died when their three boys were little in a car accident—Kit had been barely twenty.

Then her second husband had turned into a jerk and left her for another woman when Kit was a few months pregnant and was in her final year of college. So, she was a single mother with five kids in total at thirty.

"Any particular reason things are good?" Amanda smiled at her. She knew the signs that Kit was in love.

"Just kind of met someone. Maybe this could work out," Kit whispered, so their mother didn't hear. Their mother was always overly interested in her kids' love lives.

"Congrats. I won't ask too much. But now I want to." Amanda glanced at their mom, who was suddenly looking their way. Like she knew the sisters were sharing a secret.

Kit let out a laugh. Her little sister was definitely happy. Maybe at Christmas, she would bring the mystery man around. That would leave just her without a significant other for the holiday.

Of course, the thought of Christmas stopped Amanda. By Christmas, she would no longer be pregnant. By Christmas, her life would be back to normal, or at least a new normal.

"Mandy, have you been putting on weight again?" Her mom was studying her from across the room.

"Mom, leave her alone," Julia, the baby, said from by the stove.

"Yeah, Mom." Kit's tone was harsh as she defended her.

"Mom's right." Amanda looked at her tall, thin sisters and saw what her mom saw: Amanda not measuring up. "I have picked up a few pounds this year. I have to get on a good diet."

"No, you don't," Julia said firmly. "Don't let anyone tell you how you should look, Mandy."

"Thanks, Julia," Mandy said, trying not to cry. Her sisters were the best.

Kit put her arms around her and tried to hug her. Amanda pulled away, not wanting her to feel just how fat she had gotten, and said, "I'll just go to the ladies room. If you'll excuse me."

Once in the bathroom, she put the lid down on the toilet and sat down. Knowing it was coming and having it said were two different things. The words hurt so much more than the knowledge that someone thought that way about her.

She loved her mom and would spend every moment she could with her, but her mom knew what words were spinning around in her head and said them out loud. Even when those words were true, they still hurt.

She stayed in the bathroom until the tears stopped, then she stayed just because she didn't want to face everyone yet. Here she was sitting in a bathroom crying on her baby's only thanksgiving. The thought brought another set of tears.

A knock came on the door. Wiping her tears, she said to whoever was on the other side of the door, "I'm in here."

"I know. Can I come in?" Tess asked.

"It's open." Amanda scrubbed her face with a hand towel to try to get the look of crying off her face, but she didn't move from her place on the toilet seat.

Tess came into the small room and sat down on the edge of the tub. "Kit told me what your mom said."

The tears came again at the memory. "I know I'm fat. I know I'm getting fatter. I don't need someone telling me I'm fat … reminding me."

"You're not fat, Mandy." Tess took her hand that was not wiping the tears from her eyes. "You're just built differently from your sisters."

"I've always been bigger than them."

"We all gain weight. I know I have."

"You were pregnant." Amanda knew how hypocritical she was. That was the reason she was gaining weight also.

Except it was completely different since Tess had a baby to show for all her weight gain. Amanda would have nothing in the end. Just extra pounds that would take a long time to shed—if she ever did.

"I know, but I gained more than I should have. I gain weight easily too."

"No, you don't, you barely eat." Amanda had eaten with the woman enough to know she ate the littlest bites and always stopped eating once the first person at the table was done.

"Have I ever told you why I don't eat much?"

"No."

"Because when I was five, I almost died," her friend said. Amanda hadn't heard her talk much about her life when she was younger. "I almost died of starvation."

"No, you didn't," Amanda stated, as if Tess would lie to her.

"Yes. Where we lived, it was sometimes hard to make money, and other times impossible. No money meant no food," Tess explained from her spot on the tub.

"But that doesn't happen anymore," Amanda argued.

"In Russia, it does," Tess stated firmly.

"I always forget you weren't raised here," Amanda whispered.

"So, I eat like I do because I cannot control my eating. I do not feel full, so I have to control how much I eat," Tess further explained.

"I'm sorry. I didn't know."

"I do not want your sorries. I just want you to understand. We all have something." Tess handed her another tissue.

"I'm sorry I haven't been there for you and the baby. It's just been hard for me this time," Amanda admitted in the small bathroom, looking at the floor at her feet and not her friend.

"Mathias told me about your babies. I didn't know. He only told me after book club on Sunday. He should have told me months ago." Tess took Amanda's hand in hers.

"I should have told you," Amanda whispered.

"No, you don't need to talk about it. He knew and just let me think you were mad about the baby and didn't like me anymore." Tess looked angrily at the door, as if Math was just on the outside and could hear her disappointment in him.

"I really like you, Tess. You're the best sister-in-law I have. Not that the last one was steep competition," Amanda admitted with a smile.

"Can you talk about it? I don't think Math knows everything. Just what he has overheard over the years. It wasn't happening to him, so he didn't care too much as it was happening."

No, I don't want to talk about it! Amanda's mind screamed. But instead, she asked, "What do you want to know?"

"All of it." Tess was still holding her hand.

"Okay … I can't carry a pregnancy to term. I lose the baby before twenty-five weeks. They are stillborn, always." Amanda got stuck on the word. She didn't want to tell her baby what was going to happen to it. To let it know about its death sentence.

"How many?" Tess asked quietly.

"Nine, but don't tell my mom. She doesn't know about them all." The number was always hard to say. "I don't have an issue getting pregnant, but it's always been this way."

"Mandy, that is a lot." The look of shock on Tess's face made Amanda want to cry again.

"I know. Maybe it's because I'm getting older, but it's bothering me more. I mean, I knew when I was thirty, I would never have a baby of my own, but now at close to forty, it's becoming so real." The real reason was that this was the last baby she would carry. She would never let this happen again.

"Then I accidentally get pregnant with Mathias's baby. And now Ruth," Tess said, as if she had realized the reason Amanda was depressed. Most of it was the truth.

"I'll get over it. After the holidays, I'm going to work to get over it." This would all be over after the holidays, if not way before then.

"How did you handle working in the maternity ward? Babies every day?" Tess asked.

"That's work. I can work with them. I love them. But now it's personal; it's harder. I know I wasn't there for Kit with the last two like I had been with the first three." Knowing she had hurt her sister over the past few years hurt Amanda, though her sister had never let on that she was bothered by it.

"I think she understands. I think they all do, and now I will. I'm not going to push you with the baby. You do what you want. If you don't want to hold her, then don't. I will understand." She knew Tess was lying. She knew Tess wanted her to be involved with the baby.

"Thank you, but I have to force myself. She'll only be a baby once, so I should enjoy it." It was the truth, but actually doing it was going to be the hard part.

"I want you to be Zia's godmother," Tess blurted out.

"What? No." Amanda met her eyes.

"Yes. You are my friend and Mathias's sister. I want it to be you."

"I would be honored. I have never been one before." She faked a smile. One day, it would be real, but not today.

"What? With all these nieces and nephews?" Tess questioned.

"I think most of them were avoiding the situation. When all the kids were born, except Kit's little ones, I was in the middle of it. I think I turned them all down at one point. Back then, I couldn't." She just hoped she could now.

"I only request one day in January, and then you can do what you want with it." Tess got up and hugged her.

"That's after the holidays, so I will have my head together by then." Amanda smiled.

"Just give it time, Mandy. Sometimes you just need time." Tess stood up.

"I need to leave the bathroom, don't I?" Amanda asked her.

"Yes, but take your time. No rush. Your parents have another bathroom," Tess said as she slipped out the door.

Amanda stood up and washed her face in cold water, trying to get the puffiness to go down. Looking into her own face, she saw she was tired, pale, and her face was a lot rounder than it used to be. She looked old and fat, that was for sure. Why had her mom invited Hue today? She didn't need him to see her old and fat too. But he saw her four days ago, and she was old and fat that day also. And what happened in her kitchen had all been in her imagination, nothing real.

Opening the door, she walked out of the bathroom and went to the living room where her father was, and probably a brother. She was not ready to see her mom just yet. It was likely to be a long day of avoidances.

CHAPTER 9

HUE WAS WATCHING the pregame show with Math and his dad, Otto, when Amanda came into the room. She was cute in her orange pants that hugged her curves and her oversized Landstad Tigers sweatshirt she suddenly wore all the time. She was really into school spirit now that she was back.

From his spot on the couch, he couldn't tell she had been crying, but the murmurs and whispers said she was. She sat on the other end of the couch from him and turned her attention to the TV. But she had sat in his line of sight, so he could analyze her from his position and pretend to watch TV. The show he had been watching had lost all his interest.

So far, he hadn't heard what her mom had said, but it had sent Amanda into the bathroom for over an hour. It must have been something big. As he watched her, she pulled her legs up under her. Turning her body away from him, she leaned her head against the back of the couch. He loved when she sat like that. She did it when they talked during games on her couch, but she'd face him then.

It made him want to pull her into his arms and hold her as they watched the game. Make her feel better. But he knew she would most likely be mad if he did something like that in front of her family.

Soon, Tess brought her a stiff drink. He watched as she took a sip, then put it on the coffee table and leaned her head back again. Before the kickoff, Math went and got them all another beer, and when he came back, he handed out the beers and then gave his big sister a little side hug before he sat down. It warmed his heart that her siblings were making an effort to make her feel better, but it still hurt that he couldn't.

Math started to ask him questions and make comments about the game that had started, but Hue wasn't overly interested in what was happening beyond the woman at the end of the couch. She was in pain, and he could see it on her.

At one point, Julia came and sat next to her and whispered something to her, but Hue hadn't heard what was said. Amanda nodded, and Julia went back to the kitchen. The football game continued behind her, unseen.

Kit announced the turkey was ready, and everyone jumped to their feet, except Amanda, who barely moved. Her dad and brother left the room quickly since they were there for the food.

Alone in the room, Hue walked up to where she was sitting. "Time to eat, Nordskov." He held out his hand to help her up.

Turning to him, she took his hand, and he pulled her to her feet. Then he continued pulling until she was in his arms. Hugging her tight, he felt the tension in her body. He also felt her soft curves and an electric current that was always there when he touched her. Just an innocent hug had his body coming alive.

Letting her go, he held her hand as they went to the table. All the chairs were full when they got to the dining room except two. They weren't even close to each other. Amanda moved to the chair furthest from her mother, so he was next to Julia and her mom for the meal. Not exactly where he wanted to be, but he was happy he was at least there.

Conversations floated around the room as the group ate. But he was watching Amanda on the other end of the table, and she wasn't talking to anyone. Just eating, but not really doing that either.

Julia leaned toward him and said, "Mom called her fat."

His eyes shot to her, watching her picking at her food. He wanted to yell at the woman who had given her life. Amanda was not fat. Amanda was Amanda. She wouldn't be who she was if she was tall and skinny like her sisters. She was bubbly and fun, and he wanted to caress every one of those curves.

"Why?" Holding back his anger, he questioned her little sister.

"Because she's Mom. She can always tell what your weakness is, and she pokes it." Julie handed him the rolls.

"But she's not even fat. She is bigger than you and Kit, but everybody is," he said.

"I am going to take that as a compliment. For all of us. Thanks, Hue." Julie handed him the mashed potatoes.

"Where's Kyle?" he asked about her husband.

"Work. He didn't want to have to make me come back so he could work tomorrow. I get the entire weekend here." She smiled. She was the one sibling who didn't get to come home as often as the others. It had been months since he had seen her.

"I hope you have some fun."

"I'm going to. We're going on a trail ride tomorrow," Julia told him as she handed him the stuffing.

"We?" he asked

"Just the siblings." Then she laughed. "No kids. Just Tess, I guess. You should come. The more, the merrier. Just no kids."

Julia had three girls that Hue could only pick out at the table because they were girls.. Since Kit had only boys, Julia only had girls, and he knew Math's kids well. He always knew whose kids were whose when they were all together.

"I would like that. What time?" he asked, because Amanda was sure to be there, and where Amanda was, Hue wanted to be.

"Early. I hope that Mandy is out of her funk tomorrow." Julia looked down the table at her sister, who was excusing herself. Nobody else seemed to notice.

"Me too," he said, and his attention was taken by two of Kit's older boys, who started to argue about something.

By the time the meal was over, Hue knew Amanda had left. Julia had been talking to Kit at her other side, and they agreed that she was too depressed to stay. He tried not to listen, but his ears strained to hear what they were saying.

Kit leaned toward her sister and whispered, "I cannot believe your mother."

"Oh, *now* she's my mother." Julia rolled her eyes at her sister.

"She's always been harder on Mandy than anyone else about her weight. I mean, I'm thirty pounds heavier than I was before James was born, but she hasn't said boo," Kit was saying.

"She just notices it on her because we are shaped the same. We're built like dad. AKA, we carry it better," Julia said.

"I guess." Kit only shrugged.

"It doesn't help that she's in her depression cycle," Julia commented.

Hue wondered what they meant by that. Did she have depression and he never even knew? But if Math didn't know, Hue didn't know. He was hating that he had to get all his information about Amanda from her brother.

"I know. I think the baby dug that up," Kit agreed.

"Maybe it's the holidays. She was kind of like this last year too," Julia went on.

"I was pregnant with James then, so maybe that was why," Kit stated.

"Do you think it's that again? It's been years," Julia replied cryptically.

"Baby Zia is in her face all the time. She's friends with Tess, and Math is her brother. Maybe it's too much for her. After her distance with Josiah, I didn't even try to push with James. I could tell it was bothering her." Kit scooted her empty plate away.

"Do you think she'll go by the cemetery?" Julie questioned.

"No. Mom says she's never been there. Mandy would be so happy today if, you know ..." Kit sighed.

"I know. She would be ten this year, a few months younger than your Jacob," Julie said about one of Kit's boys.

Kit was silent for a few moments as their mom tried to get in on the conversation, but neither sister let her. So, she busied herself with something else before the sisters started talking again.

With a sigh, Kit said, "I don't know if giving her space is the way to go. Or if being on her so that she has to talk about it is better. You never know with Mandy."

"What are you two whispering about over there?" Math interrupted the conversation.

"You making an honest woman out of Tess," Kit shot back at him.

"I just bet." Math let it drop. That was his usual response to his getting married.

Beside him, the sisters got up and started taking dirty dishes off the table, their conversation over. Soon, the men were back in front of the TV, but for Hue, trying to watch the game was impossible. Sadly, the game held no interest to him with Amanda gone.

As soon as the game was over, he made his excuses and left the family get-together. It didn't hold as much appeal without Amanda. As he walked across the lawn, he heard his name being called.

Turning, he saw Math jogging toward him. "You're leaving so soon?" Math asked in confusion.

"Yeah, just not feeling right today."

"Sure, it happens. Julia said she invited you to the trail ride."

"Is that okay?" he asked, suddenly wondering if he was getting too much family time. That they might be getting sick of him.

"Yeah, it'll be fun. You can ride with Mandy. She's coming. I got two favors to ask you, though." Math's eyes were off in the distance, not on Hue.

"What?" Hue asked.

"First, Tess and I want you to be the godfather of Zia." Math surprised him. With his other kids, Math had given that honor to family members. So, him choosing Hue was an honor, especially since Tess came from a large family, and this was her first child.

"Me, a godfather? I'm not even in the mafia." He laughed at his joke, and Math rolled his eyes.

"Yes, you. Tess talked to Mandy this morning, so it's all set. The baptism will be sometime in January." Math rubbed his hands together. To warm them or because his evil plan was now in motion, Hue didn't know.

"I would be happy to." He had never been a godparent before.

"Good, that's what I wanted to hear." Math smiled back at the house.

"What else?"

"Could you stop in and see Mandy when you get back? She let Mom get to her today," Math said.

"Yeah, I will. She looked depressed," Hue agreed.

"Yeah, she gets this way sometimes. Sometimes babies get her down," Math admitted, finally hinting about Amanda's depression. If Hue didn't already know, he might not have picked up on it.

"I know how she feels," Hue admitted about himself.

"Shoot, man, I forgot. I'm sorry. I've been so into the whole new baby thing, I forgot about you." His friend had been there when Hue had needed to talk when infertility got to be too much.

"It's okay. I'm excited for you and Tess. I'll stop by and see Mandy." His heart jumped a little at the thought of seeing her one more time today.

"Thanks, I owe you one. And don't forget about tomorrow."

"I won't." Hue got into his pickup and headed to town. Heading to see Amanda again, with her brother's permission.

Or maybe more importantly, *without* her brother's interruption.

CHAPTER 10

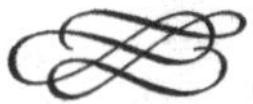

AMANDA DIDN'T KNOW how long she had been sleeping when she woke up. When she had crawled into bed after shedding her clothes, she pulled the covers over her head. After leaving her mom's in the middle of the meal, she had gone straight from car to bed and didn't even stop to cry again. She just let sleep take away the pain. It had worked, she realized as her eyes opened.

The sight that greeted her upon opening them was Hue sitting on the edge of her bed, barely touching her as he ran his hand over her hair. When his eyes met hers, the softness of his made her want to burrow into his strong arms.

"How are you?" he asked quietly.

Naked, was all she could think. After all, she *was* completely naked under the covers. Instead, she said, "Fine."

"You had me worried today. I don't like to see you as sad as you were." He continued to run his hand over her hair, causing her entire body to tingle. Pregnancy hormones.

"My mom," was all she could say, then bit her lip to stop it from quivering as memories of earlier that day came back to her.

"Your mom is wrong, Mandy. You are perfect." His hand went from her hair to run down the side of her face and across her jaw. A touch so light she almost didn't feel it, except it left a trail of heat as it went.

"She's right. I am getting fat again."

"Don't say that, Mandy." His fingers ran over her lips. His hand left her face, and he pulled out his phone, pushed a few buttons and put it down on her nightstand. Turning back to her, he whispered, "I am going to kiss you, and I don't want your brother calling to stop me again."

Before she could ask what he was talking about, his mouth touched hers. Just a light kiss that made her think of soft, fluffy snowflakes falling from the sky onto her lips, only warmer—much, much warmer]. His hand went around the back of her head and pulled it up a little as he deepened the kiss.

Pulling her arms from under the cover, where they had been trapped, she was able to run her fingers through his auburn hair and pull him deeper into the kiss, opening to his tongue's request. Everything inside her was hoping this wasn't another one of her dreams.

She knew she should stop, because if it wasn't a dream, it was Hue kissing her. Wouldn't kissing him ruin his friendship with her brother or something? Wasn't this off-limits?

As the kiss intensified, she stopped caring about her brother and let herself be thoroughly swept away by his friend. Sitting up, she couldn't get enough of the man. It was suddenly as if his kisses were needed to keep her alive. His hand ran down her bare back, exposed by her movement. When her hands slid out of his hair and down his chest, he groaned as she bunched his shirt in her fists, keeping him close.

Needing more of him, she tugged the shirt over his head, their lips parting for the first time. His eyes held hers as she tossed his shirt on the floor. It was only then, when he wasn't kissing her, that doubts flooded her mind.

"Don't stop." Her breath was ragged as she begged.

"There is no way I'm going to stop." His eyes broke from hers and dipped down her body. It was then she realized the blankets had all fallen, and he was looking at her bare breasts. Finally, someone else could enjoy them.

Grinning widely, he cupped them, and his rough thumbs grazed across her nipples, making her moan and push them further into his hands. He took the hint and placed hot, wet kisses down her neck and across her chest until he was circling her nipple with his tongue. She bit her lip at the pure, breathtaking bliss of the sensations it was causing, but she couldn't hold back a second moan as he took the entire nipple into his mouth. Pregnancy hormones were the best.

Unable to look away, she watched his mouth on her breast, which made the sensations pound through her even harder, hotter. Making her wetter and wetter. When he slid across to the other breast, her arms that were holding her up gave out, and she was flat on her back.

His mouth left her nipple with a pop as he asked, "You, okay?"

"No." She breathed out the word, and when he started to pull away, she grabbed him, "I am so far from okay I can't even see it from here."

His low chuckle was followed by his hand sliding down over her stomach. Her breath hitched at his actions and her inability to stop him because she didn't want him touching her stomach. Any place else was just perfect. But he didn't stop, nor did he pull away.

His rough hand continued down over her hips and kept going. As his hand moved, he groaned. "Are you completely naked, Mandy?"

Shifting, she whispered, "Yes," as his hand finally slid through her wet folds. If she could think at all, she would be embarrassed by how wet she was.

His mouth took her nipple back as his fingers easily found her clit, making her gasp at the pure bliss of the feelings. With his fingers and tongue working their magic on her body, she let go of any thought she might have had and focused on Hue's touch.

A deft thumb was circling her clit with just the right pressure. Moaning in appreciation, she lost any control she once had when he eased a finger into her. Before long, he added a second, causing her body to start to shake uncontrollably. She knew she was about to come.

He must have sensed it also because his mouth left the breast he had been lavishing his attention on, and he looked up into her eyes. She had been watching his mouth on her breast, letting the image of Hue's lips on her skin make her even hotter. A lazy smile was all she saw until an orgasm sent her over the edge, and her vision dimmed. Moaning and shaking her head, Mandy let sensation after sensation wash over her in waves.

Moments later, she lay sated while she watched him stand, slide out of his jeans and underwear, and climb back into bed with her, finally as naked as she was. Watching him reveal muscle after muscle was better than any of the hundreds of dreams she had had about him lately. Far better. Even his massive erection exceeded her dreams.

Before he got back into bed, he looked her over slowly. Her immediate reaction was to pull the covers that had slid away over her body. To cover it. Except he had already seen it all, touched it all. And he was still there, still wanting more.

"God, you're beautiful, Mandy." His voice was husky. This time, they were skin to skin as he pressed himself to her.

Blushing at his words, she couldn't say anything as he kissed her cheek and chest, knowing they were probably bright red. His hands ran over her thighs and hips in reverence.

"Do you have protection?" he paused in his kissing to ask. "I didn't think I needed any today."

"Fuck." She groaned and fell back onto her back. It had been months since she'd needed condoms and never in her apartment since she'd moved. "I don't. But it's okay, isn't it? I mean, you can't …" She couldn't finish, hating to bring up that he was shooting blanks.

"Are you sure? I mean, I know I can't get you pregnant, but there are other things condoms are used for." He leaned over her as he spoke, and he was blushing as bad as she usually did.

Reaching for her phone on the nightstand, she explained, "I am clean. I can show you on my phone, I have the information—"

His laughing stopped her by pulling her hand back to him as he said, "I'm fine with your words. Only you would be able to produce a report. It's the doctor in you."

"I'm not a doctor; it's just that my records are on my phone," she argued.

"If you're not a doctor, and I am not a doctor, why are we both naked?"

"We're not at the clinic."

He looked around the room and back at her. "How about that. Not the clinic. Just the doctor naked in her bed."

"Nurse practitioner," she corrected, running a hand over his chest and flat stomach, feeling his muscles contract at her touch.

He hissed in a breath. "Whatever, the important part is you're naked and sexy as hell."

Instead of arguing, she slid her hand over his cock, causing him to groan, but that only emboldened her as she slipped her hand over the silky texture of his steel shaft. In her hands, she reveled at the size and shape and everything about it. Only now realizing what he had been hiding in his pants for so long.

Her hand slid up and down, only pausing to run a thumb over the tip, and she couldn't seem to stop. That was until he jerked away from her with a click of the tongue. "No more. I can't take it."

Chuckling, she let her hand fall away, but she stopped as he shimmied down her body, kissing a trail from her breasts, across her stomach, and right to the pulsing nerve bundle that was her clit. As his tongue raked over it, she gasped his name. But when he sucked it into his mouth, her hips jerked off the bed, her body unable to control its own movements. Two long fingers slipped into her as his mouth continued, and she couldn't stop the orgasm from rolling through her, over and over again with his name on her lips.

She barely noticed his smirk as he kissed his way up her body again, still pulsing from what he had done. When his mouth claimed hers, she was lost in his kiss. So lost that when he settled between her legs and just looked at her for a moment, she looked back. She loved being with him, here in her bed.

With an ever so slight shift, his erection pressed into her. Eyes wide, she looked down between them as he slowly slid into her. She could feel him filling her, but the sight was incredible. When he was completely encased, he stopped and let her adjust.

When he didn't move, she looked away from their joining and saw he was looking at her face. Blushing again, she whispered. "It fit."

Laughing, he kissed her lips as his hips started to move, thrusting slowly in and out. Pulling his mouth from hers, he shakily asked, "You didn't think it would?"

"I just have never encountered anything that—" she groaned as he shifted, sliding even deeper into her "—big."

"Thank you." Smirking, he bent down and kissed her nose.

"Jerk," she growled as she grabbed his firm ass and forced his speed to increase. That was all the encouragement he needed to pump into her.

Meeting his every thrust, she knew she wasn't going to last. Being with a man who knew his way around the bedroom with her pregnancy hormones, there was no way she wasn't coming fast.

As her orgasm overtook her again, she felt him giving way to his. As he pumped hard into her, she threw her head back and chanted his name as waves of pleasure washed over her.

Lying under his heavy, hot body, she couldn't contain the smile on her lips. That was hot. Hue was hot. That was amazing. She would have to find a way to bottle pregnancy hormones. She would never have to work again if she could sell this feeling.

He rolled off her, pulling her with him so that they were facing each other. Their legs were still tangled, and his hand was resting on her hip until it slid up her body and into her hair, pulling her lips to his for a hard kiss.

"Can I tell your brother you're okay?" he asked, his breathing still ragged.

Shaking her head, she told him, "Maybe let's not bring up my brother right now."

"Okay," he agreed and then cupped her breast, kneading it gently. "I'm really the biggest you've ever had?"

She pushed him away from her as she blushed, but he pulled her back in his arms. "I knew you would bring that up. I only said that in the heat of passion."

"I love when you blush, and now I know it covers your breasts. And they're amazing." He bent down and kissed each of her breasts that were still red.

"Don't get used to them. They're not always this big." Realizing what she said, she stopped breathing. How was she going to write that one off? He must not have noticed what she had said because he continued to kiss her breast.

"Do you always sleep naked?" He kissed up to her neck and nuzzled just under her ear.

"Yes." She could barely say the word.

"Since you moved in across from me? Naked?" He pulled back to look at her.

"Yes, I get hot at night." Shrugging, she didn't need to explain this to him, did she?

A grin spread across his face. "I can see that. You make me hot too."

"Shut up." She laughed at him and pushed him away again.

He let himself fall and pulled her with him, so she was above him. "Which one don't you believe? That you are hot or that I am hot for you?"

"Either one. You don't even notice me." She tried to keep her tone light, but she knew he didn't think of her like that.

"I always notice you, Nordskov." He ran his hands through her hair and cupped her face. "Why do you think I like to watch sports with a sleeping woman? Because she is you."

"I don't sleep." The protest slipped out before she could stop it.

"Resting your eyes, then. And sometime snoring." He kissed her nose.

"Now I know you're lying." She laughed. She had been caught.

"I am so glad your brother asked me to check on you. And that you leave your door unlocked." He rolled them back, so they were facing each other again.

"I was told it was an invitation to come in once." Running her hands up his chest, she marveled at his muscles. That she was allowed to touch them.

"So, I came in. I did knock, you just didn't answer." He tapped her nose with his finger.

"Sorry." She tried to bite it but missed.

"You were resting your eyes." Chuckling at her, he yawned.

"That I was." She smiled down at him.

"You're adorable when you sleep. Have I ever told you that?" His eyes were closing as he said it.

"No. Maybe if you had, you would have got here faster." She touched his cheek. "Are you falling asleep?"

"Yes, I assume you will too in a moment." He pulled her to him.

"Nope, I'm wired now. Most people fall asleep, but not me. It's like an adrenaline rush, and I take a while to come down."

"You, who can sleep at the drop of a hat?" His eyes were open but just barely.

"That's why I have so many speeding tickets from you. Post-sex speeding." Instantly, she wanted to reel them back in, she didn't need him to know why she had been speeding all those months ago.

"Then I will go hide your car keys." He turned her in his arms and pulled her tight against his body. She felt he was staking his claim on her.

"Goodnight, Hue."

"Goodnight, Nordskov."

As she felt him fall into a steady breathing pattern, she lay in his arms, loving the feel of his arms around her. Cursing herself for telling him about the speeding tickets. He'd given her three tickets and way more warnings before that in the seven months she kept going back to Paul. In other counties, she could usually get out of the tickets by claiming it was a medical emergency, but Hue knew her, and she couldn't lie to him.

Snuggling closer to his warm body, she tried not to think about the fact that she was lying to him every day by not telling him she was pregnant. But until tonight, she didn't think he cared beyond her being Math's sister. Now she had no idea what to do about what was happening between them.

She was starting to show, so she almost had to tell him. Really showing, not just extra weight around the middle. Maybe if his wife had ever conceived, he would have noticed that her stomach was harder than it should be. Maybe since he had never seen her naked, he didn't notice her body was different, like she saw it.

What she didn't want to do was turn this happy, excited feeling she had when she was with him into the sad depression that was her life. He was a bright spot in her life right now, and she needed it.

Sleep overtook her as his warmth seeped into her, giving way to her constant exhaustion. She resolved to just live day to day with Hue, forgetting about the future and the past when she was with him. Just let herself be happy for a little while before life came crashing back to her.

CHAPTER 11

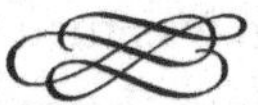

THE TRAIL RIDE WAS FUN, except he had the wrong Nordskov sister behind him on the four-wheeler. It was Julia whose body periodically brushed him as he drove behind Kit. The bright spot was that Amanda was sitting behind Kit, so he had a perfect view of her being jostled around.

To make it even better, she was constantly telling Kit to slow down or not to hit so many potholes. He could hear her words from where he was. To make her point, she would occasionally hit Kit's shoulder.

The other bad thing was that it was twenty degrees, and it had snowed a little overnight. It was colder than he thought it would be—another reason he would have liked the heat of Amanda holding on to him.

Hue was on the last of the three four-wheeler train, with Math and Tess in the lead. They had been out for around two hours and were heading back since Tess needed to feed the baby soon. They had left the infant with Math's older kids. The oldest was sixteen.

In front of him, Kit slammed on the brakes and turned off the machine. Climbing off, she started to walk away, yelling, "You drive it if I'm so bad at it!"

"No, Kit, you drive. I will walk. Go just as fast as you want to—not that I was stopping you before!" Amanda shouted as she climbed off the machine.

Turning, Kit yelled back, "I am driving just as fast as Math is. That is how it works!"

"No, you were hitting every bump you could, even when I asked you not to!" Amanda yelled.

"I cannot see all the bumps, Mandy. I'm sorry," Kit said as Math circled back and shut off his machine. Tess peeked out from behind him.

"Those two," was all Julia said from behind him.

"What's going on?" Math asked his sisters, having missed the argument that had happened so far. By his confused expression, it seemed Math had missed his sister's disagreements all morning.

"Kit is driving like a maniac," Amanda accused Kit, her arms folded as she stood away from the machine.

"My driving's just fine."

Julia put her hands on his shoulders and climbed off the machine they shared. Her touch did nothing to him; no sparks, no tingles. Nothing like when he touched Amanda. And he loved being touched by Amanda.

If he had thought their first time together had been magical, it had nothing on what had taken place in her tiny shower as they got ready to come out for the trail ride. He had kissed every inch of her, all the inches he had spent months dreaming of seeing, touching, tasting. And he had gotten her to come with her back pressed to the shower wall as hot water washed over them. Twice.

Just looking at her yelling at her sister was making him want her. Her angry face was just as cute as her sleeping face. She was still arguing with her younger sister with her gloved hands on her hips, hips he had caressed that morning.

What bothered him most was that she had not wanted to reveal their relationship today. Maybe he was asking too much to tell everyone they were a couple only twelve hours after their first time together, but it was exactly what he had wanted to do. Tell everyone.

He had wanted her to ride with him, not Julia. But before he could say anything, Kit had requested Amanda ride with her. Now the woman regretted that decision.

Julia yelled at both the sisters. "I will drive, and Mandy can ride with me!"

Again?! his mind screamed. "How about I take Mandy, and we can go as slowly as she wants. I'm in the back, anyway."

"Perfect." Kit shot her sister one last angry look, then walked back to her four-wheeler.

"Works for me," Julia agreed, and they got on the machine.

Math turned back around and headed back down the trail, followed by the younger Nordskov sisters.

Driving up to Amanda, who was still standing with crossed arms, he asked, "Need a ride, Nordskov?"

"I don't know how you get by with calling me that. Every one of them are Nordskovs." She was still a little ticked off.

"No, only you and Math are. The other two go by their married names," he corrected.

She was still standing, not getting on the machine yet. "Why do you call me Nordskov? My name is Amanda. Can you say, Amanda?"

"Amanda Marie Nordskov. See, I can say the whole thing." He got off the machine and pulled her into his arms. "I call you Nordskov because when you moved back, right next to my place, I said, 'Well, if it isn't Amanda Kelly,' and you said, 'It's Nordskov.' I took that to mean you wanted to be called Nordskov all the time."

"You sometimes call me Mandy," she reminded him and kissed his chin.

"Because when I want to get you naked, I don't think Nordskov is the name I want to say." He took off his gloves so he could touch her.

"You only call me Mandy when you want me naked?" she questioned.

"Almost always," he confirmed, cupping her cold cheeks with his warm hands.

"Hue?" A slight frown crossed her face.

"What, Mandy?" He kissed her red nose that was cold under his lips.

She smirked. "Do you want me naked?"

"I always want you naked." Nodding, he pulled her closer. Just to prove his point, he rubbed his erection against her leg. He was rewarded by her laughing. And he kissed her to make her stop.

"I regret all these layers." Her words were muffled as she took off her mittens and slid her hands under his jacket.

"Even though we are in the middle of nowhere, and your siblings could come looking for you at any moment?" he said as her hands tugged at his shirt until she had it untucked and could slide her hands over his bare skin.

One of her hands reached behind him and turned off the machine. "Now we can hear them coming." Her hand went back under his shirt.

"Did you plan this?" he asked as she undid his belt.

"No, Kit does drive like a maniac. This was just a bonus." As she went onto her tiptoes and kissed him, he returned the kiss and held her head to keep her lips on his. They were cold from the freezing temperatures, but her tongue was hot and made his blood boil. Or maybe it was her hand that had found its way into his jeans and was holding his erection.

"I like bonuses." He let go of her face and watched as she freed him from his pants into the frosty air. Before he could protest that it was maybe too cold for this, he watched her take his straining cock in her warm mouth.

Leaning against the machine behind him for support, he closed his eyes—the sight was too much for him to take. It had been close to a decade since a woman had done this to him. And his ex-wife hadn't been as good at it as Amanda was. Warm hands were holding him around the waist under his jacket, keeping her hands warm. Needing to touch her, he pulled off her hat and cupped her head, tangling his fingers into her hair, not caring that in a few minutes, she would have to face her family. Because only this moment mattered right now.

Knowing he was going to come, he tapped her on the head, then he said it out loud, but still she didn't let him go. In fact, she held him tighter, her mouth moving faster as her fingers pressed into his skin.

He couldn't stop his orgasm as it rolled over him, and he watched as her mouth didn't leave his erection.

When he was done, she lifted his boxers back over his cock, zipped his pants, and redid his belt. All her concentration was on redressing him as she tucked his shirt in and lowered his jacket. Her blue eyes were bright and alert and she looked up at him, then she pulled his lips to hers and kissed him.

Wrapping his arms around her, he pulled her tight against him and lifted her off her feet, needing her as close to him as possible. Around them, the woods was quiet, and he heard nothing but her breathing. They were completely alone in the cold. A cold he couldn't feel when Amanda was in his arms.

Pushing away from him, she reached down to grab her mittens and his gloves that were beside him on the machine, and said, "We should go. Maybe that took too long."

As she handed him his gloves, he let his hands linger where they touched. "Do you want to drive or ride?"

She looked up in the air as if pondering his question. It was like nobody had ever offered the choice to her before. Her voice was excited as she quirked an eyebrow at him. "Drive."

Knowing she was going to drive, he kissed her one last time and climbed on the back of the machine. Scooting back, he helped her settle in front of him. Then he slid forward and settled his hands between her jacket and clothes, holding on to her under the jacket.

Turning the key, she said loudly, "They never let me drive."

"I hope that they don't have good reason for that." He nipped her ear as he said it.

"Moving trees," was all she said as she hit the accelerator, and they started for Math's house.

Hue hugged her closer and laughed at her answer. As they drove through the light layer of snow, he hoped none of the siblings would catch on to what had happened. Or maybe he hoped they would, so he could tell someone about this amazing woman he was falling in love with.

Amanda did not hit any trees during the trail ride, which she was proud of. They were sneaky, after all.

Math had commented on her past incidents when they had finally pulled into his yard, checking for damage as he walked around the machine. Maybe it had taken longer than it should have to get there, but she didn't regret what had taken all the time.

Being able to drive had made her less nervous about the rough conditions. It made her not think every bump was going to start a miscarriage that would be her fault. A miscarriage that would be caused by her actions and not her body's rejection.

Or maybe it was that Hue was holding her tight; he wasn't going to let anything happen to her. Or the baby, even if he didn't know it was there. Hue's arms would protect them from everything.

Waking up this morning, Amanda had wondered if it had all been a dream. That Hue Strong had not woken her from a deep sleep and made love to her. Her, Amanda. But the evidence was overwhelming with him still in her bed. Still sleeping, she had been able to watch him for a while, just enjoying the moment.

Not too long since they had to be at Math's early for the trail ride. She would have gladly passed up trail riding to spend the time with

Hue instead, if it wouldn't have caused too many questions. Whoever had planned this as a first thing in the morning activity should be punished. Amanda only had little time to enjoy the man in her bed before she had to get up.

Having him join her in the shower had been the pick-me-up she had needed. The post-sex glow had lasted past not getting to ride with Hue on the trail ride and right up to her sister trying to kill her. Well, maybe that was dramatic; her sister was only trying to kill her baby.

By the time Kit had kicked her off the machine, Amanda was well past done with her little sister's driving. At that point, she would gladly have walked back to Math's house, no matter the distance. She couldn't take another moment on that machine.

But getting to spend time alone with Hue again had been a better plan. A way better plan. And then he had let her drive back as slow as she wanted, without saying a word about it. She should have driven a bit faster to make up for the time they had spent stopped on the trail, but then Hue would have to let go of her sooner, so no way was that happening.

Now, walking into the house, she hoped they thought she was red from the cold and not because of the memories of why they were late. Now she was suddenly glad for the chilly weather this morning. Or maybe because she was out of the cold now.

"Look who made it back. I was going to send a search party," Julia said from the counter where she was helping Tess make food.

"It wasn't that long. Amanda drove," Hue said, as if that explained it all.

Julia couldn't hide her grin. "Are there any trees still standing?"

"Don't you have children to raise somewhere?" Amanda shot at her.

"Nope, I'm having my mother raise them today." Julia chuckled.

"Okay, girls, no fighting," Tess said as Math walked into the house and right into her arms.

"But, Mom, if we don't fight, we don't talk," Julia said in a nagging voice to Tess.

"Go. Everybody out of my kitchen, and go watch TV." Tess pushed

Math away and sent everyone to the living room. Math's house was not an open concept, and all the rooms were divided by walls. Usually, it was annoying, but today she liked the distance from everything.

"Me too?" Amanda asked her friend. Hue had rested his hand on her back when they stopped in the middle of the room, and now, since she was not moving, he slid it across until it was gone. She hoped nobody noticed.

"You can stay. If you don't fight. Kit already left," Tess informed her.

"I'm sorry, I was just tired of being jostled around," Amanda explained, walking to the counter to help with food preparation.

"Just saying." Tess shot her one last look.

They worked in silence, with the only noise being voices from the living room. Amanda tried not to listen for Hue's voice in the mix but couldn't help it. It was his voice she was focused on.

Tess slid a pan of uncooked lasagna into the oven and turned to Amanda. "So, you seemed to be feeling better after yesterday. Aside from how you acted toward Kit. Anything you want to talk about?"

"No," she said quickly. Too quickly. "I mean, I just finally got a good night's sleep last night, so I'm feeling better today. And I found this diet I'm going to try."

Tess leaned against the counter and shook her head at the last comment. "I'm beginning to wonder if your mom even tries to control what she says around you kids. I mean, she has a little dig for you all. You're fat, Kit's single again, Julia never comes home, Math was single and now is not married. Some days I love her, but some days …"

"It's always been that way. If there's something in your life you don't want to think about, she brings it up."

Her mom had been the negative voice in her head forever. Though Dolly was proud of all her kids, they could always be better. Dolly pushed for that. It was just how her mom was, and mostly Amanda was used to it, but some days she couldn't stop it from bothering her.

"So yesterday, your mom was trying to get Kit and Hue together. I mean, it would be a good match, him not having kids, and her having a ton. But neither were into it. Neither even noticed it was happening.

I watched her all day, trying to get them to sit together, but Julia sat next to him instead. Then after she tried to get them to take a walk, but instead, Hue left early. It was fun watching her get frustrated."

Amanda stared at her. Her mom had tried to set him up with her sister? Never once had she tried to set him up with her. Never once. What was so wrong with Amanda that she would prefer to see Hue with Kit than her? Reining in her anger, she told Tess, "The joke's on my mom. Kit's met someone. She just hasn't told Mom about it yet."

No way was she telling her friend about her and Hue last night. That was hers to know and nobody else. For now, at least.

"That's good. She needs someone in her life. I wanted to tell her that if Hue had ever had any interest in one of the girls, he would have acted on it before yesterday. I mean, he's around you guys all the time," Tess said, watching her closely.

Was it too closely?

Could Tess already know?

Looking right back into her friend's piercing eyes, she lied, "Yes, if he had been interested, it would have happened long before now."

"That's what I thought, too," Tess said as Julia came into the room.

"They're just talking sports now. Boring. What are you talking about?" Julia complained.

"Nothing much. Just your mom," Amanda said, knowing that was a topic Julia was deeply interested in. And it would get the topic away from Hue and his interest in any of the Nordskov sisters. Mainly her.

"Thanks Mandy, for taking her attention off me yesterday. Between you and Kit, she could forget that she had another daughter," Julia said, taking a carrot from the counter and biting into it.

"Your day will come," Amanda informed her.

"Oh, I know. And you will all thank me for getting her off your backs for months when she finds out Kyle left me." Julia pointed her carrot at them.

"No, Jules, really? When?" Amanda turned and hugged her sister.

It was a surprise, but not a complete shock. Though Amanda had barely liked her sister's husband, that didn't mean Julia didn't love him.

"It's been happening for a while, but this summer, he officially moved in with his girlfriend. So, I guess that is that. Sadly, I will be completely divorced before I get the nerve up to tell my mom. I remember how disappointed she was when all the rest of your marriages blew up. And I thought I would be the only one to stay married to the first person I married. But then Kyle decided he wasn't happy anymore."

"Are you going to stay in Fargo?" Tess asked from across the kitchen, letting the sisters have their hug.

"I don't know. I want to come back, but I would need a job and a place to stay. I am not staying with my parents," she said with a little laugh.

There was no room with their parents, even if she wanted to come home and bring her kids. Every weekend Kit already brought her five there so her ex could see them. Not that he usually did, but Kit always made the effort. On top of that, Julia was a high school principal, and all the area schools had one already, and openings were few and far between.

"What do you want to do?" Tess asked.

"Job-wise? I don't know. I haven't planned a lot. I have been numb for too long." Julia squeezed Amanda one more time and let her go.

"You get over that, then you'll figure it out. Maybe you want to come back here and do something else," Amanda said. Her own failed relationship had led her to coming home, and it was starting to feel like the right thing to have done.

"If you want to come back, I have a job when you want it. Nothing much, but a job." Tess was the president at the bank. It would be a big change for her sister, one she didn't think Julia was exactly ready for yet.

"Let me figure out how to tell Mom. So far, I'm going to stay. I do love my job, and the girls are happy where we are." Julia shrugged.

"What's all the chatter about in here?" Hue walked into the room, followed closely by Math.

"Nothing, just women's musings." Julia shot the other women a look.

Amanda looked at her littlest sister. She wasn't ready to tell everyone yet. It had been months since she had actually seen her brother-in-law, so it wasn't a surprise what Julia had admitted. Maybe in the future, she would go down to visit her for a weekend, have a girls weekend. Of course, it would be after everything was over, and her life could begin again. She would start fresh, like her sister. After.

Following the meal, where she didn't get to sit by Hue, they all settled in to watch a football game. It was not a good one, and Amanda fell asleep almost immediately. After a night of activity and little sleep, her exhaustion had caught up with her, and she didn't even try to pretend she wasn't going to take a nap.

When she finally woke up, she was alone in the living room, and there was a blanket over her. All she wanted to do was turn over, snuggle down, and sleep more. Instead, she heard voices in the kitchen and couldn't get comfortable again. Wondering what was going on, she got up, folded the blanket, and went in to see.

Hue and Math were sitting at the table, chatting. Tess and Julia were nowhere to be seen. Hue saw her first and smiled. "Good morning, sleepy head. Have a good nap?"

"Yes, thank you. You should have woken me up." She tried not to only look at Hue, but her brother as well.

"I learned long ago not to wake you up, Mandy," Math said with a chuckle about memories from their childhood. It had happened in this very house, and her little brother had been far worse than her sisters put together. He had spent far too many years making her life difficult.

"I don't wake up swinging anymore," Amanda said to her brother, though he'd deserved it more often than not back then.

"You were sleeping pretty deeply, so we left you. You must need it." Hue grinned at her, as if he wasn't the reason she hadn't gotten much sleep the night before.

"Where are Julia and Tess?" Looking around, she sat down at the table with them, ignoring the comment.

"Julia went to Mom's a few hours ago, and Tess is either feeding the baby or napping after feeding the baby," Math said, looking at her. Almost as closely as his girlfriend had earlier.

"What?"

Math rubbed his chin before saying, "You sleep an awful lot."

"I've had a busy week. A busy few months, for that matter." Sitting up in her chair, she folded her arms. She didn't need a lecture from her bother.

Math put his hands up in defeat. "I am just commenting, Mandy."

"Well, stop. I will live my life the way I want to. I don't tell you what to do, so don't tell me," she argued, not daring to look at Hue, though he had seen many sibling fights over the years. This was the first time she was embarrassed by him seeing one. Her brother was out of line.

"What does that mean?" Math asked.

"It means if I want to sleep, I can. In fact, I can do whatever I want, whenever I want."

"See, Hue? She's a bear when she wakes up," Math told his friend.

Amanda turned to Hue, still angry with her brother, but willing to direct that anger toward him.

Holding up his hand, he said, "I didn't say anything."

"I'm ready to go," Amanda hissed at her brother. "Tell Tess I will call her soon. And you can tell her she is dating a jerk, and I wouldn't marry you either."

"Low, Mandy," Math said as Hue ushered her out the door.

Once in the pickup cab, she took some deep breaths. It was a baseless anger, even she knew that. But her brother had more than a little of their mom in him. He, too, could find that one thing. The only positive was that he didn't call her fat and lazy, just lazy.

"Are you going to be okay, Nordskov?" Hue asked from the driver's seat, not touching her like he had on the way out this morning. She was missing that touch.

"Yes, just give me a moment." She closed her eyes to try and get her emotions under control. To try and figure out what was bothering her so much since waking up.

"I will give you the car ride. But once I get you back to your apartment, I am going to do my best to distract you." Hue smiled at her but kept both hands on the stirring wheel.

"You sound pretty confident over there that you can take my mind off Math," she said shyly.

"I hope to god that within a minute of shutting that door, you will forget you even have a brother." Hue reached over and ran a hand lightly over her hair, like he did it all the time. The touch was just what she needed.

"What brother?" she asked as his hand did it again and ran over her hair.

"I have no idea." He turned on to Main Street.

Hue parked the pickup right outside their front door, and since it was the Friday after Thanksgiving, Main Street was empty. Racing up the stairs, they didn't make it into her apartment before he had her pinned to the wall and was making her forget the entirety of her family and every friend she had ever had except him.

Later, as she made them a quick supper, he went into the hallway and stairwell to collect the clothes that had been shed getting to the apartment. Watching the almost naked man walking around her apartment, she wondered why she wasn't shouting to the world that she had herself a man? But instead, she wanted to keep him to herself, just like her baby, getting as much happiness from it as she could before it was over. Because in her heart, she knew it would end.

No matter how pretty his words were, she was just Amanda.

No matter what he said or did, in the back of her mind, she knew it was short-term. That he would get bored with her, that he would realize what she looked like, that he could do better. Because everyone in her life had. How was Hue any different?

CHAPTER 13

SUNDAY WAS LOOKING to be another great day, but he was getting to spend it with Amanda, so of course it was going to be great. Saturday they had spent together, mostly on the couch, mostly naked and mostly arguing over something until she fell asleep. Then he watched her sleep and made sure she was warm enough.

Now he was showered, shaved, and heading back to her place for another day. No Math today—he was busy with his family, so it was going to be a no-distraction day. With Amanda. Grabbing the chips, he headed out the door, just like he wanted to every Sunday. Or any day of the week, actually.

He wanted to press her about telling people about their relationship, but he knew she would have some excuse why they shouldn't. It was too soon, too new, too close to the holidays, her sister had met someone, let her have the attention for a bit ... Every excuse was believable, just to a point. It didn't matter how long it had been or who else was in a relationship. They were in a relationship. But he let it go every time.

Today he was wearing his football jersey and black shorts, like many Sundays when he didn't have to go outside in the cold. He was hoping not to be wearing them long. Opening the door, he saw her sitting at the table with papers in front of her. She was wearing her glasses. Since he had left nearly an hour before, she had put on a Landstad Tigers sweatshirt and black leggings, and she looked adorable but overdressed.

"Nordskov, what have we talked about? The home team needs you," he teased.

She looked down at her outfit. "The home team has to do without me today. My shirt is dirty."

"It is supposed to be dirty; that's where the luck lives," he explained with a grin.

Her face fell instantly, and she asked in disbelief, "Have they been losing?"

"Yes," he answered honestly, but it maybe wasn't the shirt's fault. Nothing was the shirt's fault when Amanda was wearing it.

"I think I washed the luck off your shirt." She slid off her glasses with a smile she was unable to hide.

"When?" he asked breathlessly. Mostly because she was so sexy when she did that. And even if he had made love to her a few hours ago, it was still the little things about her that were so sexy.

"Two weeks ago. That's okay, right?" Her frown was adorable.

"You have killed the season, Nordskov." He stomped over and threw the chips on the table, on her paperwork in feigned outrage.

Instantly she started looking through the chips and said with no apology, "Maybe next year, Strong."

Grabbing her out of the chair, he lifted her onto the table, and she dropped her glasses in the process. Amanda laughed at him. Lowering his head, he kissed her neck and bit it lightly as he said, "You better be lying to me."

Still laughing, she said, "Don't mess up my paperwork, Hue."

"Don't worry about that." His hand slipped under her sweatshirt, running his fingers up her sides.

"I have to." She tried to be stern but giggled. "It's my job."

"Your job is to see people naked, Nordskov." He bit her ear lightly as he said it.

She laughed again. "My only goal is to get you in my office, naked, Strong." Her hands slipped up under his shirt.

"Never, Nordskov. You will have to settle for me naked here." He groaned as her legs wrapped around him.

"One day." She sighed and unwrapped her legs from him, then pushed him away. "I really have to do this paperwork by tomorrow. I should have done it yesterday, but I got distracted by something," She looked at the ceiling for a moment. "Oh yeah, you."

Letting her go with a growl, he bent and picked up her glasses, slid them on her face, and kissed her nose. "I will let you work. The game's started."

"It's only the pregame show," Amanda said, wrinkling her nose.

"If you want to get work done, Nordskov, you cannot be making fun of the pregame show or making those cute faces." He kissed her nose again and lifted her off the table, setting her on her little feet.

Grabbing a bag of chips, he went to the couch alone. He turned on the TV and watched the pregame show for a while as he ate the chips. Every once in a while, he would look over at her, but she was always working. Glasses on, head down, and writing with her black pen.

"Are you at least going to watch the game?" he asked, wondering how long she would work.

"I should be done by then," she answered, barely looking up.

"Will you change into the shirt before the game? Before the entire team sees you?" he teased, still looking at her.

"If you go get it, I will slip it on before kickoff," she said, not looking up this time, just writing something down.

Getting up, he went into the room he had slept in for three nights now, three glorious nights. Opening her closet, he was surprised at how few clothes she had hanging in here. Most were lying in a knee-high pile on the floor. Seeing the shirt, he pulled it off the hanger, leaving the hanger hanging there with dozens of others just like it, empty.

Walking out into the main area of the apartment with it in his hand, he said, "Nordskov, you have got to do laundry. Soon, you will have to go to work naked. Not that I would care, but you should maintain a professional image when out and about. Feel free to be naked when home."

"Ha-ha. I manage to find something every day." She didn't look up as she said it, but he could see she was blushing. Maybe she was embarrassed that she didn't like to do laundry. Maybe he should offer to do her laundry, but he didn't. Since she didn't want to tell anyone about them, he didn't do her laundry.

So far, he hadn't brought up what they were to each other. He didn't want to push her, but he wanted to know. He wanted to take her outside of this apartment. Not that being alone with her wasn't great, but he wanted to share her.

Bringing the shirt over to her, he kissed the top of her head. "I like you naked."

Back at the couch, he tried to leave her alone—she wanted to work—but he kept looking over to see if she was getting done. But she just kept working. Though she missed seeing the kickoff, she had changed into the jersey with only seconds to spare as he demanded it happen from across the room. Then he willingly watched her change her shirt instead of the kickoff. Just getting a glimpse of her breast encased in a yellow bra had been worth it.

Halfway through the first half, she finally got up from the table, put the folders on the counter, and sat down next to him. Right next to him, not on the other side of the couch like she used to.

"What did I miss?" she asked.

Putting his arm around her and pulling her closer, he kissed her and said, "You don't care."

Snuggling into his body, she yawned. "You're right."

Within minutes, she was sleeping, but this time it was the first time she was sleeping in his arms during the game. It was so much better with her in his arms.

CHAPTER 14

 Not warm, but sunny. The first week in December in North Dakota was never usually warm. It was not snowing yet, but you could smell it in the air. By Friday, they would have more snow on the ground.

Amanda had been overbooking Tuesday for weeks in hopes of keeping her mind off her own body. Today she was doing pretty good. Going from patient to patient, she was distracted enough to not think about the fact that she was starting her twenty-fifth week. She examined an unusual growth on a middle-aged woman's back and didn't even think about it. Well, maybe just a little bit.

Ruth had been in this morning, first thing, and this time Amanda was ready, steeled for what was coming. It was easier when she knew what was coming. As lunch passed without her being able to eat more than a few bites on the go, she checked her appointment book and realized Sally Strong had an appointment today. Sally was Hue's mom. Sally was the mom of the man she had been sleeping with for over a week now.

Over a week.

In fact, in two days, it would be two weeks. Since they had started their relationship, she hadn't been able to crawl into bed at

7:00 p.m. and sleep for almost twelve hours. She hadn't been able to just mindlessly watch TV until she fell asleep. And she couldn't dwell on the fact that she was still pregnant; that she still hadn't lost her baby.

He didn't seem to notice that she was getting bigger in the middle. Since the first time they had sex, she had gained three pounds, mostly in the middle. He hadn't asked about it, and she hadn't told him about it. She was just enjoying him while she had him.

Did she think Hue Strong would be with her forever? Of course not. He was just there, and it was fun for now, and she would enjoy it while he was there. And enjoy it she did. Sometimes right when she walked in the door after a long day, she almost ripped his clothes off as he made them supper, or in the morning when she turned her attention right to him the moment her eyes opened. And she could let him go to sleep without something to dream about.

Pregnancy sex was the best drug she had ever known—not that she had any experience with drugs. She was hot for him morning, noon, and night. She was almost willing to overlook how those same hormones made her happy and weepy and angry all at the same time.

Since the beginning, she had not wanted to tell anyone they were sleeping together. Knowing he wanted to tell everyone made her sadder, because all she wanted to was keep him to herself. She had decided that if she spilled her guts at this weekend's book club, she would let him tell the world. If she didn't feel comfortable telling her closest friends, she wasn't ready to share with the world.

Running twenty minutes behind by the time she got to Sally's appointment, she rushed out to the waiting area and called her name. Looking up, she saw that Hue was with her. But when the woman got up, she told Hue to wait for her. His face showed disappointment, but Amanda knew Sally didn't notice.

Leading the woman away from the man who shared Amanda's bed that morning, Amanda let her into an exam room. Sitting down at the computer, Amanda typed for a bit while they talked about the weather and if there was going to be a storm this week. Both decided no, just snow.

Turning her full attention to Sally, she asked, "What have you decided?"

"I will do it. You said last time you can schedule it in Fargo, so I can be closer to Jill." Sally's attention was on her hands and not on Amanda. They had talked about everything a month before, and today, Sally just had to decide. It was past time.

"Yes, I want to schedule it soon. It won't get better, just worse." Amanda wrote herself a note about what Sally's decision was.

"Thank you, Mandy. I was really nervous about what was happening, and you made me feel better. Giving me time to think it over helped a lot." Sally patted her arm.

"I just want you to feel better." Amanda looked up at the woman who gave Hue his blue eyes and maybe red hair, but Sally's had been gray for as long as Amanda could remember. "Have you talked to Hue?"

Somehow, she knew the woman hadn't. Hue would have asked her about it, even before they had slept together. Not just because she was a nurse, but because she was his friend.

"No, I just can't talk about it with him." Her blue eyes looked at her shoes, still unable to meet hers.

"Do you want me to, without you there?" Amanda knew Hue was thinking the worst of his mother's visits with her. All she wanted to do was put his mind at ease. It wasn't as serious as Hue was making it out to be.

"No, men just don't understand," Sally stated, dismissing the entire idea.

"I think he will understand. Just because he is a man doesn't mean that he wouldn't understand that a hysterectomy is the answer to your pain," Amanda said to the woman. It was a simple procedure done every day, but recovery would be long, and that was the big issue.

"I just don't like him thinking of me that way," Sally admitted.

"I think he knows where babies come from, and that sometimes, those parts need to come out." Amanda pushed the woman a little to tell her son. Because Amanda knew she couldn't without the patient's permission, no matter how much she wanted to.

"Can you schedule it for after Christmas down there?"

"Yes, I will call you when I have a date and time," Amanda assured the woman.

"Thank you, Mandy. I look forward to hearing from you." Sally Strong got up and walked out of the office.

Amanda leaned back in her chair. Hue was going to be asking, and she couldn't say anything. Again.

Her next appointment was her last for the day. It was after five already, and she was ready to drop. Just get through one more. Out in the waiting area, she called out the name of her last remaining appointment, but nobody got up. In fact, the room was empty, except Hue was sitting there still. His mother must have left without him.

Today he was wearing jeans and a brown sweater for the chilly day. He was wearing cowboy boots she hadn't seen on him before. Catching her eye as he stood up, he walked over and said, "I don't think they're here."

"I can see that." She turned and put the file on the desk in the room. Her desk was in the lobby since she didn't have a receptionist. There was no budget for one this year.

"Can I talk to you?" he asked, putting his hands on her shoulders and starting to rub them.

"If it's about your mom, no." She tensed as she said the words and his hands stopped moving.

"Why not?" He dropped his hands.

"Because she is a patient," she explained. Again.

"I share your bed," he stated, as if that mattered at all.

"Doesn't matter. I asked if she wanted me to talk to you. She didn't." Amanda tried to convince him.

"I thought since we were sleeping together you would bend your rules a little."

"Really, doctor-patient confidentiality is not my rule. I have to follow that one pretty close. Especially here where everyone knows everyone's business. You in my bed makes no difference; you know that." She put her hands on her hips.

"She is my mother." He pointed out, as if she didn't know.

"Then have her tell you." She tried not to let her anger get the best of her.

"She won't talk to me," he said, though she already knew that.

"Ask Jill. I know she knows," she told him, giving him the back door to the information. But if he would just talk to his sister, she would tell him everything, everything Amanda couldn't.

"So, you know something?" he demanded.

"Of course, I know. She is my patient," she admitted, but he already knew that.

"Another secret that you won't tell anyone," he spat out.

"What does that mean?" She knew what he was getting at. She could feel her bubble of happiness popping, and she couldn't stop it.

"You won't tell anyone about us. Are you ashamed of us? Of me?"

"Of course not. I just want ..." She could say what she really wanted. Things not to change? The world not to catch up with her? To not think toward the future?

"What you want is always what it is. What about me and what I want?" He took a step back and yelled at her.

"What do you want?"

"You, and to tell people about you and me. To tell my mom that I am bringing someone to Christmas. To tell Math anything about why I want to spend all my time with his sister. To start planning a future together!"

"I can't give you a future right now. I want to, but I just can't."

"When then?" he demanded of her.

"I don't have a date I can give you." She told him the truth. As long as she was still pregnant, she couldn't think of the future. Because that future wasn't going to include the baby she was carrying, and she didn't want to think about that. She never wanted to think about that.

"So, you think that I want to keep this secret until who knows when? To pretend I don't have feelings for you when we are in public? Oh, wait, we don't go out in public, do we?" Running his hands over his face, she could see his anger.

"Yes. And it's too much to ask." She knew that it was, even she could see that.

"Yes, it is, Amanda Nordskov. I don't want to do that anymore. I don't want to be your dirty little secret."

"I understand." Suddenly, she was freezing in the little waiting room. She tried not to shake with the chill that came over her.

At that moment, she understood everything. She had ruined what they had and had done it in a matter of days. Any feelings he might have had for her were gone, if they had ever been there. Because Amanda hadn't given them time and room to grow.

Instead, she had let her emotions focus on the baby she carried when she should have been putting all her attention on making her relationship with Hue grow. She had messed everything up.

"Yeah, I didn't think you would try to keep us together. Sometimes showing a little emotion would be helpful." He turned and walked out the door. She watched as he turned to go upstairs to his apartment.

She slipped off the white coat she wore home and laid it on the chair near her. Without a backward glance, she shut off the lights as she went out the door, locked it, and went up to her apartment. For the first time in a week and a half, she walked in the door and stripped down as she walked to her bed. Once naked, she crawled in and shivered in the cold blankets.

That was when she let the tears fall and let the sobs overtake her. She knew he would end it one day, but he had done it on a Tuesday. Why did it have to be a Tuesday?

She could still smell him on the sheets. Burying her nose in the pillow, she curled into a ball of pain and let the tears consume her. For one night, she would let the pain of losing Hue overwhelm her. Then she would get back to preparing for the pain of losing the baby she still carried, still wouldn't admit to herself she desperately wanted.

CHAPTER 15

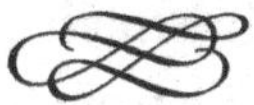

IT WAS SNOWING big fat flakes covering everything in a thick blanket, and Hue wondered if it was snowing in Landstad tonight. He knew Amanda loved snow on Christmas ever since she was a kid. He resisted the urge to text her to see if it was snowing there. It had been almost three weeks since he had blown up at her.

The moment his anger dissipated, he wanted to apologize. But when he thought of what he should say, he couldn't figure out what he would apologize for. After all, it was her who wanted to keep their relationship secret. She was the one who had been so secretive about his mother.

In the three weeks, he had seen her a total of three times. Twice had been in passing, and once had been when he was on a date. Math had set him up with that woman from the bank Tess had wanted to set him up with. With no reason to say no and not wanting to make Math think something was up, he had gone.

The woman was from the next town over, and Hue had seen her around town before, but he had never talked to her. She was nice and friendly, and they had a lot in common, but she wasn't Amanda. It seemed he wasn't right for her either because she had been okay with not seeing each other again.

He had taken her to the bar and, of course, Mia and Amanda came in. The date had been a disaster, even before Amanda had shown up, but seeing the pain on her face had sealed the deal. The cousins had not stayed more than a few minutes, but the damage was done. The two of them had departed at the end of the night and had not seen each other since. Neither had wanted another chance.

Now it was Christmas day, and he was at his sister's house in Fargo, as far from the Nordskov Christmas as possible. He didn't need to spend an evening across the table from her or even in the same town as her. Instead, he was spending it with Jill's four kids and her husband's family. The house was packed, but there was not a lot of fun and laughter, not like Thanksgiving had been. They weren't even watching the football game because Jill's middle two had been in a dance recital, and everyone was watching the video Jill's husband Dan had taken. Again.

He found his way into the kitchen because he didn't want to watch it the first time—a clip would have been enough. He found his sister busy getting lunch together. These were the times she reminded him of his mom when she was busy in the kitchen. Maybe it was sexist, but the kitchen was where Sally Strong thrived.

Grabbing a pop from the refrigerator and leaning against the counter, he asked, "Do you need help?"

"Not from you. I want everything edible," she joked.

"I can cook. I have been living alone for three years now, and I've survived." So, he only knew how to read the back of boxes. Who cared? Everything came in a box.

"Barely, by the looks of you." Jill looked him up and down.

"Thanks."

"Hey, you're the one who just watches TV and avoids people. Why did you even come?" Jill dug in the fridge for something. He didn't help, because she had been mean to him.

"You asked me to come," he reminded her.

"You rarely come. You usually just go to Math's house and pretend to be a Nordskov for a day," Jill pointed out.

"I wanted to spend the holiday with my sister." Hue grinned at her.

He hadn't spent a lot of holidays with his younger sister since his ex and her did not get along. He shouldn't have let that stop him from visiting his family, but he had. Hue was starting to see that his ex-wife hadn't gotten along with many of his friends and family. Why hadn't he noticed that when they were married?

"Bull. Something's up." Jill set down something a little too hard.

"Nothing is up," he argued.

"Yes, it is. You're acting just like you did when Krystal kicked you out. So, I'm assuming it's a woman."

"Not a woman." He shook his head.

"A man?" Jill asked with a smirk.

"Jill, it's nothing. Definitely not a man." He rolled his eyes at her.

"No, a woman. Is she from Landstad? Mom didn't say you were seeing anyone." Jill leaned toward him in excitement.

Sighing, he said, "Mom doesn't know, so don't tell her. And yes, she is from town."

Jill quit actually making lunch to lean against the counter across form him. "Do I know her?"

"Yes, you most likely know her." Everybody knew everybody else, and both had lived there since childhood.

"No hints? I have to guess?" she asked.

"Maybe you just don't need to know."

"I need to know, Hue. This is the woman who broke your heart." She smirked again.

"She didn't break my heart," he grumbled.

"Your heart's broken. Twenty questions?" she asked, a game they used to play when they were kids all the time.

"Fine. But you are already down two. From Landstad, and Mom doesn't know." He wasn't going to let her cheat. She was a known cheat from way back.

"Older or younger than me?"

"Older." His sister was barely thirty.

"Always been there or came back, or God forbid, new?" That made him smile because she was right about the number of new people in town. Aside from Tess, he couldn't name five people that had been there less than five years.

"Came back." Just over a year. A great year. Until three weeks ago.

"What color hair?" She pointed to her own brown locks.

"Blonde." Gorgeous, soft blonde hair.

"What does she do?" Jill tapped her chin as she questioned.

"I won't answer that. You have to ask either-or questions." He wasn't going to let her cheat.

"So, there is only one in town of what she does," Jill surmised.

"Yes." He sighed.

"Which is the Nordskov girl that moved home recently? It has to be one of the sisters." She was talking to herself as he watched her work her way through the question. "Wait, only two are technically older than me. Kit is my age, but would you know she is actually older? I'm going with the oldest one. Cannot remember her name. What is her name?" She wasn't asking him, but the ceiling, as if it had the answers.

"I am not reminding you." Hue didn't want to say it.

"And you are not denying it. I win." She grinned and threw her fists in the air as if she did actually win.

Hue rolled his eyes. "You don't win; you don't know her name."

"I win. I'm going to go ask Mom what her name is. She will know." Jill started to leave the kitchen.

"Don't ask Mom, please." He stopped his sister.

Jill turned back to him. "Then tell me, Hue. What is the name of the Nordskov girl that has you all moody and sad? The one that broke your heart?"

"Mandy," was all he said, missing her even more as he said the name.

"Yes, that's it. Mandy. Isn't she a doctor or something? Mom sees her." Jill hugged him and then went back to making lunch.

"It doesn't matter. Whatever it was is over. Mom does see her."

"I know. Mom said she set up the surgery for after the holidays, so she wouldn't have to miss the time with the family. And she set it up for down here, so I can take care of her," Jill said, as if Hue had any idea his mom was having surgery.

"What surgery?" Hue demanded. Why was his mom's health everybody's secret?

"Mom didn't tell you?" Jill stopped and looked at him in confusion.

"No, and neither did Mandy." He couldn't help but sound mad.

"Well, Mandy can't. Her job and all." Jill looked at him closely. "You thought she could, didn't you? But I know you know she couldn't. She's a doctor, Hue."

"She's a nurse practitioner. We were close. She could have told me. She's my mom," he reminded his sister, who should know all this already.

"No, even if you were married, she couldn't tell you. Doctor-patient confidentiality," Jill reminded him, same as Amanda.

"She's my mom."

"Doesn't matter. Mom is having a hysterectomy on the eighteenth. She is probably embarrassed to tell you since you're a guy and her son and shouldn't be thinking about her uterus, or so she thinks. For the last few months, she's been having pain. Your Mandy suggested it. The pain will get progressively worse and then she will have to have it done. Right now, it is more preventative. Your Mandy even made the appointment down here, so she can stay with us for a few weeks, so as not to bother you so much. Probably because she knows you're a jerk, and Mom shouldn't have to recover with you." Jill informed him of everything Amanda had done for his mom, and all he had done was yell at her.

"I thought she had cancer," he admitted. "And nobody was going to tell me."

"Not every medical situation is cancer," Jill said. "So, Mandy. Mandy and Hue. Can that be saved?"

"I don't know. I was pretty awful to her. It's been a couple weeks, and I haven't really seen her. Quite the feat since we live across the hallway from each other."

"How about a big old sorry? It usually goes a long way for women, and maybe chocolate. Don't do flowers—we women don't actually love those."

"I think it is too late for that," Hue admitted sadly.

"It's never too late," Jill said optimistically.

"There were other things too. Not just the mom thing."

His sister sighed. "There always is."

"She didn't want to tell anyone we were seeing each other." He could finally tell someone.

"Ever?" she asked, surprised.

"It had only been just over a week, but she didn't want Math to know, and she hadn't told any of her friends."

"Did you ask her why?" Jill started to make the sandwiches again.

"She really didn't say. Everybody says that she gets depressed over the holidays. Maybe it was that?" He remembered that after the fight. After he had walked away from her.

"And you dumped her over the holidays? Smooth move, brother." Jill threw a bun at him, missing.

"I just kind of went off on her," he admitted.

"Why did you want to tell everyone? It had only been a week."

"I wanted everyone to know." That was how he was.

"Why? You could have waited until after the holidays and had a few weeks of just you time. Let the world pass by. Why was it so important to tell everyone right away?" Jill turned to him.

"Because, at Thanksgiving, her mom said something to her. It was mean and hurt her bad. We sat on the couch together, and I couldn't comfort her. I wanted to hold her and make her feel better, but I had no right to in front of her family. I still don't."

"You could have just hugged her. You're practically family. Did any of her family members hug her? Talk to her?" she asked as she laid out the lunch meats on a tray.

"Yes, they all did." He remembered seeing almost all the siblings hug her at least once.

"So maybe you could have done the same. Now, if you started making out on the couch, people would talk. Though, I have never been to a Nordskov holiday, so maybe it's acceptable." She laughed.

He laughed at her joke. It felt good to laugh again. "I guess you're right."

"I know I'm right," Jill said as their mom came into the room.

The conversation turned back to the recital, and Hue tuned it out. What he couldn't tune out was his sister's words about Amanda. Was she right? Should he have just enjoyed their alone time and let Amanda set the pace of the relationship? What was the difference between them being together alone or with the entire town? It was maybe nice to not be the topic of gossip in the beginning.

"Hue? Are you listening?" his mom was asking him.

"What? Yes," he said.

Jill was grinning at him. "Mom thinks you should pursue Mandy Nordskov."

"She is such a nice girl. Well, she's of course, a woman." His mom started helping his sister with lunch.

"Yes, she is nice," Hue confirmed.

"I am so glad she came back," she said to Hue and then turned to Jill. "She's divorced. She married right out of college, and that lasted for years. But now she is single, and so is Hue."

"Mom." Hue tried to get his mom to stop.

"I wonder why the marriage broke up?" his sister asked, looking at Hue.

"He cheated," his mom gossiped. "And after everything she had gone through, too."

"What? I hadn't heard anything." Jill winked at him as she prodded his mom for information.

"She kept having miscarriages. And the one time she carried long enough for them to say it was a baby, it was stillborn. That was years ago. They even had a funeral for it. Only family, so I didn't go." The words made Hue hurt for his Mandy.

"Do you remember when?" Jill pressed.

"No, I can't remember. But around this time of the year, I think. I remember thinking it would make the holidays hard for her and her family way back when it happened. Losing someone close to the holidays is always hard."

The conversation he had overheard at Thanksgiving between her sisters became fully formed. Not all of her pregnancies had ended early—one had lasted long enough to give her hope. But that, too, had been snatched from her. During the holidays. Causing her depression during those same holidays.

"That is so sad, and during the holidays. I hope she never gets dumped around the holidays. That would be the worst." Jill shot him a look.

"What are you talking about, Jill?" his mom asked in confusion.

"Nothing, Mom. So, how are you feeling?" his sister asked.

"Good, great," his mom stated, and Hue knew she was lying because he was there. A man, after all.

He wandered back to the living room to see if the game was on, but they were watching some older dance recital when he got there. More dancing. He longed to be sitting on his couch, watching the game with Amanda beside him. Sleeping.

Was she sleeping on her parents' couch right now? Was she talking to her sisters in the kitchen? When was he going to stop thinking about her all the time?

His phone rang in his pocket. Maybe it was her. Pulling it out, he saw it was a Nordskov, but not the one he wanted to talk to, to see.

"Math," he said, answering the phone as he went to the bedroom he had been assigned for the two days he was at Jill's house.

"Hue, glad I got you. I need a favor." No small talk, no nothing.

Remembering the last time Math had asked him to do a favor was the night he finally got into Amanda's bed. And it had been as amazing as he had imagined. He would willingly do that favor over and over again.

"Sure."

"If Mandy needs to go somewhere, could you jump her car?" The temps were dipping below zero tonight, but not so cold that her car shouldn't start.

"Why wouldn't her car start?" he asked in confusion.

"I don't know. She's just suddenly nervous that it will not start," Math explained.

"And why can't you do it?" Hue knew it made more sense that he did it—they lived in the same building—but Math was her brother, and Hue was nothing to her anymore.

"We are in Minnesota for the holidays," he said. Tess's family was from the other side of Minnesota. "Mom and Dad came with us. Mom practically forced Tess's family to invite her so that she could see where she came from. Mom's being nosy. So anyway, nobody will be around for a few days. Mandy called, all nervous about her car not starting."

"I can help, but I'm in Fargo until tomorrow." He should have stayed home. Then he thought why? So, he can start her car if she needs it started? To stand by and wait for her to want something?

"That's fine. We have to get together soon. I haven't seen you in a while," Math said.

It was the truth. He hadn't made a point to see any Nordskovs in weeks. Not since he had walked out on Amanda. He had even declined offers from Math and had taken on extra shifts at work. But he wasn't going to let his failed relationship with Amanda destroy his friendship with her brother.

"The holidays," was all he said. Blaming it on that and not the fact that his sister broke his heart.

"Yeah, it's been one of those years," Math said, though his year was full of happiness.

"So, if you guys and your parents are in Minnesota, did you already have Christmas?"

"Yeah, last weekend. Of course, Mandy was on call and had an emergency and didn't make it, but everyone else came. Kit brought home her new man. He might be a keeper. He put up with all those boys like he had been doing forever. Treated her like she hung the moon, too. I liked him. And Julia finally admitted that she and Kyle were getting a divorce." Math went on about the wrong sister.

Hue had stopped listening to Math when he stopped talking about Mandy. That she had skipped Christmas with her family. He didn't think she was on call as much as she always said she was. It was an easy excuse, and everyone always bought it. Why wouldn't it be better to be with her family than being alone? And now she was alone for the actual holiday. Alone and needing to have her car started.

"That's good to hear. She deserves a good one," Hue replied.

"She does. I was hoping you would step up, but you never showed interest in her." Math laughed

"Kit?" Hue questioned. He had never looked at her that way, not even when they were in high school. She was always just Math's sister. Somehow, Amanda was able to be both Math's sister and sexy hot at the same time.

"Yeah, Kit," Math repeated. "Who else would you be interested in?"

"Not my type, Math," he said, knowing she was his type once. Before his other sister grabbed his attention.

"Since when?" Math laughed.

"Never mind," Hue stated firmly.

"No way. Have you met someone? I know the thing with Sheila was a disaster."

Hue realized that was the bank lady's name. He had already forgotten. In fact, he had forgotten by the next day.

"No, just no," Hue said.

"Tess is calling. I have to go. I will quiz you later on this." Math hung up the phone.

He tossed his phone on the bed that was his for two days. Now Math was suspicious of him. He had hated hiding his relationship from Math. He had always told Math everything, and he wanted to tell Math that he had fallen for his sister, fallen hard for the woman. He didn't even think Math would be upset, just happy for them. Except Amanda didn't want him to know. Or anyone else.

CHAPTER 16

WHY DIDN'T they just make New Year's Eve a holiday, so people didn't have to waste time working when nobody was there? Amanda sat in her empty waiting room, waiting for 5:00 p.m. to show up. Another half an hour, and she could go home.

Today her feet were killing her, her back was stiff, and all she wanted to do was eat. But she had eaten her lunch hours ago, and she had nothing in the clinic to eat. Why didn't she keep more here for snacking? Not that she needed snacking food, she was gaining weight without it.

This week she hit week twenty-eight. Her stomach had actually popped. She could now rest her arms on top of it and had started to when she was alone. No one had ever told her how comfortable it was to have a built-in armrest. But around others, she focused on not doing it.

Also, at twenty-eight weeks, she had carried this baby longer than any other baby she had carried. A baby was considered viable if she had been born at twenty-four weeks. Not that that was anything to pin her hopes on—that baby had been dead at birth. There was still no hope for a live birth this time around, either. No number of added weeks would change that.

Since Hue had left, she had tried not to be depressed and had tried to bring herself out of her funk. But nothing worked. There had been three book club nights. The schedule had been completely messed up by the holidays, so they were doing them on the off week so they could all have the holiday weekends free. But even those nights had only been fun for a few hours, then the depression came back the moment she was alone.

Skipping early Christmas with her family had been a hard choice, but as she put clothes on, nothing made her feel anything but fat. So instead of putting up with her mom, she invented an emergency and skipped it. Sleeping through the entire holiday. It was the same way she had spent the actual holiday—two days in bed. With an occasional movie that she slept through.

She was well aware she was sleeping too much. All she did was eat, work, and sleep. She barely went out. The one time she did, drinks with Mia, she got to see Hue on a date. A week after they broke up. At least she had been able to leave without Mia getting suspicious. Only three other times had she seen him around town. She didn't know if he saw her or if he just didn't acknowledge her.

He had gotten over her so easily. A week. And here she was, over three weeks later, and she still woke up and reached for him in the morning. Still picked up her phone to send him a text. Still loved him so much it hurt.

It hurt that she was so easy to get over. That their relationship had meant so little to him but so much to her. Maybe if she hadn't been in this limbo with the baby, they could still be together. Maybe even be happy. The limbo had made the relationship impossible. Or was the limbo just her excuse? Maybe she was the one with the problem. Why couldn't she be happy?

"You look like shit, Mandy." Mia stood in front of her.

"You scared me to death." Amanda's hand flew to her heart at the sight of her cousin. How had she gotten past the bell on the door without Amanda hearing? How long had she been standing there?

"I didn't sneak in here. You were lost in your own little world." Mia pulled a chair from the waiting area to the desk.

"Just daydreaming, I guess," Amanda mumbled.

"I figured you were bored in here. So, I brought this?" Pulling out a bottle of whiskey, Mia grinned. Mia's favorite alcohol was whiskey. Her cousin felt it was the answer to all life's woes. And also, all of life's celebrations.

Rolling her eyes at her cousin and her bottle, she said, "I am working."

Mia laughed at her answer as she looked around the completely empty reception area. "Do you have cups?"

Amanda retrieved Styrofoam cups from by the coffee machine and returned to the desk with them. Mia filled them and set one in front of each of them. Amanda looked at hers. There was more alcohol in it then there was usually coffee. "I can't drink while working."

Looking at the clock, Mia said, "It will wait twenty-five minutes. Then you can drink it."

Picking it up and pushing it further away from her, so she didn't spill it, Amanda asked, "How are you, Mia?"

"Let's put it this way, I am drinking at my doctor's office. My life had so much going for it, and now I am stuck in this town. I was supposed to be getting out before the new year." She drank half of her cup as she complained.

"I am not a doctor. And you have until tomorrow," Amanda pointed out. Mia had always said she'd leave by the new year. That was tomorrow.

"I've given up. This town has me, and I can't escape it. It has its hooks in me." Mia used her fingers to mimic hooks.

"You are a Landstad Tiger, Mia, through and through. You won't be happy anywhere else." Now that they were adults, a Tiger was no longer just the school mascot, but now meant that you still lived in Landstad. Depending on if you stayed or left determined if it was a positive or negative term. As someone who came home, Amanda embraced it now.

"I want to go places, see the world." Mia leaned back in her chair. "Instead, I'm a waitress."

"You're a business owner. You have been for five years now. That is more than just a waitress. But if you want to travel, do it. Take a week off and go somewhere. Better yet, take two off and see many places. Just because you live here doesn't mean you can't leave. Just come back." Amanda hated to see her cousin depressed with her life. Mia had worked at the cafe for years before buying it. She had the perfect personality for what she did. Everyone loved going in to see her.

"Alone?" Mia raised an eyebrow.

"Mia, you're never alone. A stranger is just a friend you haven't met yet. It's your personality," Amanda pointed out.

"I am always alone. And lonely." Mia finished her glass and poured another one.

"I know what you're going through," Amanda admitted.

"We should move in together, then we wouldn't be alone. Get some cats." Mia grinned at her.

"You're allergic to cats, and you're not really my type." Amanda laughed at the image of them living together.

"What? Because I'm a girl or because I'm your cousin?" Mia laughed as she said it.

"Both." Amanda shook her head at her.

"I love you too. I think you're my favorite. It used to be Julia because she's my age, but now it's you because you're the funny one."

"Thanks, always the funny one." Amanda picked up the glass of alcohol and smelled it, then set it back down.

"Mandy, you're more than funny; you are smart and pretty for a girl I am related to, and so not my type," Mia said with a laugh.

"Thanks. I know what I am. I let Kit and Julia be the pretty ones." Amanda moved the glass again, this time toward Mia in case she accidentally drank it. In her mood, she just might.

"Well, don't. They're nothing special. So, they are tall and have all that long blonde hair in perfect waves. We are sexy with our stupid mom hips even though we're not moms." Mia slapped hers. She had inherited the same hips Amanda had since their moms were sisters.

"It's more than that. I just always seem frumpy when I'm around them." It was something she had never said out loud. But if anyone could understand, it was Mia, who had five sisters who didn't get the hips either.

"You're not. You're Mandy. And if someone cannot appreciate Mandy for who she is, they don't deserve Mandy." Mia drank another drink.

"Thank you, Mia. You really should travel. Maybe this summer, we can go somewhere together. Road trip," Amanda suggested, knowing that by summer this would all be behind her.

"I can drink to that. And it's after five, so you can to." Mia held up her glass for a toast.

Amanda picked up the glass and tapped it against Mia's. Bringing it to her lips, she smelled the alcohol she had been avoiding for over four months now. She should drink it. Mia was watching her. She had to drink it, Mia was watching. She couldn't drink it, even if Mia was watching.

They set their glasses down at the same time. Mia was staring at Amanda's glass. It was still completely full. Then her eyes met her cousin's. "I knew it. I knew it. I haven't seen you drink in forever."

"I'm just taking a break from alcohol." Amanda tried to pass it off as nothing.

"Nope, you're knocked up." Mia shook her head.

"No," she lied, because she couldn't bring herself to admit it. Even now.

"Yes, yes, you are. Now, why are you not telling anyone?" Mia leaned back in her chair and stared at her alcohol, suddenly forgotten.

"Because I'm just going to miscarry it, and I don't want to have people knowing. Everyone knowing." Amanda had said it out loud to somebody, finally.

"Maybe not. This one could be fine," Mia protested.

"Mia, I have had nine miscarriages. Nine. This one is no different. There is no other outcome for me," Amanda said, wanting to drink the whiskey so bad. Wanting it to numb the pain.

"I didn't know it was so many. I had heard three or four." Mia closed her eyes.

"No. I just have to wait for my body to reject it, then I will mourn the loss. Then I will go on with my life. Then it will be ten." Amanda had never said it that way. So matter-of-factly.

"Wouldn't it be better, easier, if your mom knew? If Kit knew? Julia? Tess? Someone?"

"No. She knew for the first eight. The last one, she didn't. It was better when I didn't get asked about it after it happened. The calls of 'how are you doing?' The sad eyes when they look at me, the pity. It's easier to do this alone."

"I assume the last one was the one your mom didn't know about."

"Yes. It was the only one after the divorce."

"So, not Seth's. The doctor's?" Mia asked.

Amanda had known that her secret affair with Paul had gotten out in her family. What she didn't know was that people outside her immediate family knew. Though, to be honest, Mia was able to find out anything about anyone.

"Yes, it was Paul's. He was happy when I lost it," she admitted, ashamed he was the father of this one also.

"When was it?" Mia finished her glass and picked up Amanda's.

"Just before I moved here. That's why I had to leave Grand Forks. I needed to get away from him." Amanda told her the truth.

"That sucks."

"Yeah, it does."

"So, you're just going to wait? You're not seeing a doctor? Trying to keep it?" Mia questioned.

"The last time I miscarried, I was at work. I was in the neonatal intensive care unit. There was nothing that could have been done. I was in the only place that could have done anything, and there was nothing to be done. So, I wait."

"Do I know the dad?" Mia leaned on the desk.

"No, and at this point, I don't consider him anything but a sperm donor. This baby is mine alone to love until it is over." Amanda touched her stomach lightly, still not daring to fully touch it in front of others.

"Does Hue know?" Mia asked. Mia always knew what was happening in this town, even when you worked hard to hide it from her. Though she was happy this was the first time she had brought it up.

"No, he never realized while we were together. It's not his, so I won't tell him." And he would never know it even happened.

"Maybe it would be better with someone by your side," Mia pointed out.

"No, I'm fine," Amanda said firmly.

"No, you're not. Everyone is worried about you. Everyone sees you're depressed. You don't do anything anymore. And now I know it is going to get worse before it gets better. Way worse." There was concern in her voice.

"It's not anything I haven't been through before. I will survive this too." Amanda tried to calm her concern.

"How long do you think you have before …?" Mia asked, nodding at her stomach.

"Very soon, any day. I'm hoping before the baptism." It was in eleven days.

"How are you going to do the baptism either way?" Mia questioned.

"It's going to be the hardest day of my life. But I love Tess, Math, and Zia too much to not do it. I'll regret it forever if I back out," Amanda admitted. But in truth, she didn't know how she was going to go to the baptism still pregnant. She hadn't been able to look at that baby in weeks. She just reminded her of what she was going to be missing.

"Are you going to tell the book club?" Both knew the first rule of book club: what happens at book club stays in book club. But that was only if it was told to book club.

"No. Some things I don't like to share." If she had wanted to, she would have by now.

"You mean basically everything. Maybe Tess wouldn't have set Hue up if she had a clue that you were hot for him," Mia pointed out. Now Amanda knew that Mia had noticed everything that night at the bar.

"I am not hot for Hue," Amanda argued.

"Okay, right. I guess you're not going to want me to tell anyone either."

"Please don't, Mia," Amanda pleaded, giving up her pretense that she didn't care.

"I won't as long as you call me when it happens. So, I can cry with you. You need someone to cry with, Amanda Nordskov. To be there for you." Mia got up and went around the desk and hugged her cousin tight.

"I will call, I promise." But in reality, she didn't think she would. Her pain was never easy to share.

CHAPTER 17

ZIA'S BAPTISM morning was another cold, sunny morning. The temperatures were at minus fifteen degrees when Amanda's parents picked her up outside of her apartment. There was a thick blanket of snow covering all the land, except those spots where man had fought against nature and shoveled it into piles.

Amanda had taken great care to find an outfit for today. Leggings were her go-to pants now. She had ordered a shirt a few weeks ago, and it perfectly covered her growing mid-section in a floral pattern meant to distract. As her dad drove the short distance to the church, she was actually happy today—after a long, stern lecture to herself this morning before she even got out of bed that this only happened once, and she needed to enjoy it. She promised herself that she wasn't going to be sad on that one and only day. By this afternoon, she would have a goddaughter. At least it was some kind of daughter. It was the best she could hope for.

The parking lot at the church was full, as to be expected for her niece's big day. Her dad, Otto, dropped her mom and her off right in front of the front door. Which made Amanda happy because her coat didn't even come close to closing anymore, and she couldn't even try. Holding the present in front of her open coat, she stepped into the warm church. It was familiar in a comforting sort of way since she, too, had been baptized there as a baby.

Everyone turned to see who the new arrivals were, and she smiled at her family and friends gathered there. One of her nephews grabbed the present from her arms and took off, most likely taking it to the basement, where there would be a little party after the service. But she missed the large package immediately. Now there was nothing to distract eyes from her body.

Her brother grabbed her mom's coat, and Amanda shrugged hers off and handed it to him also. Now was the moment. Would anyone notice how much bigger she was? Would her mom comment on it?

To her surprise, her mom looked her up and down but said nothing, just smiled before she turned and walked away. Relief rushed through her. If her mom didn't say anything, nobody would. Had one of her siblings talked to her? Amanda knew it didn't matter; all she cared about was that nothing had been said.

Mia rushed over to her and put her arm around her to lead her into the sanctuary. "How are you today?" Mia asked quietly, concern in her eyes.

Today Mia was in jeans and a red sweater. She looked nothing but comfortable, but then again, she didn't have to stand in front of all her relatives and friends and be stared at. Amanda wasn't so lucky.

"I'm great. I'm so excited to be a godmother," she whispered back, though it wasn't a secret.

"A fairy godmother?" Mia asked with a chuckle.

"When her birthday rolls around, you bet." She smiled. It was like she woke up this morning and a fog had lifted, and she could be happy again. It felt good.

"You have to sit up by Math's family. And Hue." Mia looked toward the front of the church.

Following her gaze, she saw the back of Hue's head sitting beside her brother. His hair was shorter than it had been a few weeks ago. He must have gotten it cut for the baptism. She wanted to run her fingers through it, see if it felt different shorter, but she knew she couldn't. He was over her.

"Can I sit with you for a while?" she said, depression finding its way back into her heart.

"Yes." Mia led her to the pew Mia's family always sat in, and so far, her parents weren't there yet.

Hue turned around and looked at her the moment she stepped into the sanctuary, as if he could sense she was there. Their eyes met for a moment before he turned back to the front. The look said he was over her ... if he had ever been into her at all.

"You haven't called," Mia whispered.

"I haven't needed to yet." Amanda told the truth. If she made it to Tuesday, she would be thirty weeks. She knew she should be calling her former boss, Dr. David Bennett, who was a specialist in high-risk pregnancies. *Tuesday*, she promised herself, hoping that this week she would have the courage make that call. Unlike every other week before.

"That's good, isn't it?" Mia questioned with a hand squeeze.

"Just making it harder in the end." Amanda admitted, a truth she had known since the beginning, so many months before.

"Hey, you two. I need to talk to you in Natalie's escape hatch," Hazel Abbot said to them in a church whisper, which was barely quieter than her actual voice, and walked away. The cousins exchanged a look and got up without another word, following the younger woman. Hazel was recently married to the preacher, who would be baptizing the baby today. When they got to the room in the basement where, over the previous summer, their friend Natalie had shimmied out the only window. All in order to run off on her wedding.

Today Natalie was the only one beside Hazel who was there, though Amanda assumed the entire book club was coming. Both Natalie and Hazel were leaning against the lone table in the room, a prime location, given there were no chairs in it. Amanda longed to be sitting again; her back had been bothering her for a few hours today. A new symptom of her pregnancy she had never experienced before.

"You're still in here?" Mia teased the tall black-haired woman who was younger than Amanda by over a decade.

"Ha ha, I have only gone out that window once. And never again," Natalie said with a smile. A big smile, because on her next wedding day, which was already in the planning, there was no way she was leaving.

"We'll see at the next wedding," Amanda couldn't not it say, but everyone in the room knew there was no way she was leaving Sam behind.

Ruth came rushing in, still wearing her winter jacket. "Am I late?"

"No, Tess isn't here yet," Hazel said, finally sliding up on the table to sit, causing nothing but jealousy from Amanda.

"What are we doing? Kidnapping the baby?" Amanda had no idea why they were needing to meet, and her feet joined in on her back's protest of being on her feet.

"No, we're having a meeting," Natalie said.

Tess rushed in the door and closed it. "I am here."

"Finally." Natalie jumped off the table. "We need to toast the baby."

"The baby isn't here," Mia pointed out.

"Okay, we are toasting another big celebration of the group. To not let these times go by without celebrating, even if it is just a little. I think we have to get together before each one and just have a group hug," Hazel said.

"You are so sweet, Haze." Mia sniffed back a tear and hugged the blonde woman.

"So, in honor of this being an event in Tess's life, Hazel and I went with Vodka," Natalie said.

Everyone laughed. It was Tess's drink of choice. Which was not a surprise with her family's Russian roots.

Hazel started handing out shot glasses of clear liquid to everyone. Except Ruth, who she gave a shot of some kind of juice because of her pregnancy.

"Should you be drinking, Tess?" Ruth asked, knowing her friend was breastfeeding.

"I think one little shot will be okay. Need to build up her tolerance for the stuff anyway. Just don't tell my nurse about it." She winked at Amanda and, suddenly, Amanda missed them being close.

Looking at the glass in her hand, she swirled it around as the group chatted for a minute. She had to drink it. She didn't want to drink it. It wasn't that much. She had been so careful since she found out.

"To the book club." Natalie held up her glass and everyone joined in.

The group agreed and drank, except Amanda, who tried but just couldn't. As she lowered her glass in defeat, Mia grabbed it from her. Mia grinned at her, telling the rest of the group, "Looks like it was too harsh for Mandy. You know she isn't a vodka drinker." Then she drank the entire thing, as if there was a little bit left. Her face grimaced at the taste.

Once the alcohol was gone, she watched her cousin laugh and chat with the rest of the group. Amanda wiped a tear away. Mia was her favorite, too.

"Hey, we have to get upstairs." Ruth looked at the clock behind them. Since the summer, someone had put a battery in the thing, so it had the correct time for the first time in decades.

As the group disassembled, Amanda hugged her cousin as a thank you. As they walked up the stairs, Mia held her hand and squeezed it before letting her go since Amanda had to sit by Hue for this.

Knowing she was in love with Hue was hard. Sitting down next to the man who didn't love her was even harder. The happiness she had woken up with was all but gone now. She just had to make it through the next hour or so.

She desperately wanted to touch him, to just look at him. She did neither. Just sitting watching Pastor Ruston talk had her stomach churning, and the longer she sat there, the worse it got. Was it Hue's presence or something else entirely?

The service was short, and, as they stood in front of the entire church, she was glad she didn't have to hold the baby. But she did have to look at her sweet little face. And she had to look at Hue's handsome one and see that he wouldn't look at her. His eyes weren't on the baby but on the carpet below his feet. He didn't want to be there either because he made sure his red tie was straight on his white shirt three times.

Once it was over, he surprised her by helping her to her seat and sat next to her again. This time closer, and his gray slacks touched her leg as they sat. At the feeling of his leg touching hers, the familiar sensations rushed through her body, ones she hadn't felt since he had left her. Those sensations didn't diminish her rolling stomach, though.

When the service was over, they went to the basement for lunch, but Amanda knew she wouldn't be able to eat. Her stomach was almost in pain from the churning it had done during the service. Standing and moving around was making it worse and not better like she hoped. She needed to get home and lie down.

Pulling Tess aside, she asked if they could get pictures done so she could leave, explaining the stomach pains. She hoped her friend didn't think she was just leaving because she was still depressed, that she wasn't even trying to be a good godmother from the beginning.

Tess agreed reluctantly and mumbled a few words Amanda didn't even recognize before getting the group together for pictures. As they stood together for Kit and her camera, smiling was nearly impossible with the steady dull pain. Though, as the camera flashed, it turned instantly into one hard pain—a pain that Amanda was well aware of the meaning. Because she had felt that pain before, too many times before.

Excusing herself, she rushed to the bathroom to get away from people and confirm what she already knew. In the small room, she forced herself not to cry because good godmothers don't cry at baptisms.

After a quick check, she was glad she wasn't bleeding yet. It was coming, though.

Since the church was only four blocks from her apartment, she decided she would walk home and get her car and head to Grand Forks. It would take longer to find someone to drive her home than to just walk back. She took deep breaths as she left the bathroom and headed straight for her coat, not looking around, focusing on her task.

Then she was out the door before she had the coat on. There was no time.

Ice-cold wind overtook her immediately, but she forced herself to ignore it. Her concentration was on getting to her apartment. When she got there, she would have to go upstairs and get her keys. Though she had been waiting for this, she really wasn't ready. Why had she not driven? Yes, had been easier to catch a ride, but she knew this was coming. Why hadn't she been ready?

Pulling her coat closer to her body, she just wished it could have happened tomorrow, last week, last month, or four months ago. Not baptism day. Now she would have to remember the baby she lost the day she became Zia's godmother. Forever.

Fighting back tears, she kept walking. Two blocks down, two to go. *Just keep walking, Amanda*, she demanded. *Keep walking.*

"What the hell are you doing, Nordskov? It's fifteen below out, and you'll have frostbite before you even get home." Hue was in his pickup, slowly driving beside her. She hadn't even heard him coming, but she didn't care at this point. She needed to get home.

"Going home." She didn't turn to look at him. She was on a mission.

"I can see that. Get in the car." He stopped his pickup.

"Got to get home." She kept walking, ignoring him. Her focus was on her plan.

He sped away and slammed on his breaks a few yards in front of her. Getting out of the vehicle, he walked toward her, but she kept on her steady pace to her apartment. When he was three feet from her, another contraction hit, harder than the one she'd had by the cake. Instantly, she dropped to the ground with the pain. God, it hurt so much. The pain in her body, as well as the pain from her knowing this baby was dead, too. That it was over.

"Amanda?" Hue dropped to his knees by her. "What's wrong? Mandy, talk to me."

As the pain subsided, she started to get up, and he picked her up and ran her to his pickup. Putting her in the passenger seat, she curled into a ball, holding her stomach. The tears she had been unable to hold back were now streaming down her face, or maybe they had been there the entire time.

Slamming the door shut as he got in, he threw the pickup in gear. "Mandy, what's wrong? Where to?"

"My place. I have to get my car and go to Grand Forks," she said from her ball in his passenger seat.

"Hell no. I will take you if that's where you need to go." He slammed the gas pedal down as they flew past their apartment building. They must have been going close to fifty miles per hour through downtown.

"I can do it," she protested, but they were already out of town.

"I am driving, Nordskov."

"Don't yell at me!" she yelled back.

"What am I supposed to do? You ran out of that church like your pants were on fire. They wanted you there, and you couldn't stay the entire time."

"I was there. I did everything but eat."

"Barely. I was there too."

"I was fine. I was ready." She remembered the happiness she had felt that morning. Excitement. She started to cry again.

"Keep telling yourself that. So, when are you going to get over this? Are you going to be like this if they have another one? When your other friends have a baby?" His eyes were on the road in front of them. They were going far faster than the posted limit.

"Tomorrow, I will have to start getting over it. Now I have a date to tell you. Tomorrow," she whispered through her tears. Because tomorrow it was going to be over, her time with her baby over forever. Just like every other time.

"You don't think I was sitting there thinking about all the babies I never got? You don't have the market cornered on the what-ifs. I got some too." He blew through a stop sign—he didn't even slow down for it.

"I'm sorry I haven't been thinking of you having a hard time with it, too. I'm so sorry," she said, adding tears for him to her own.

"I know my emotions are not as tied to babies as yours since I never actually had one. You didn't tell me that one was born late enough to live." He reached over and touched her hair.

"She was born dead. She never lived. I was twenty-four weeks, but she still died. Her name was Layla. She would be ten now. I lost her a week before Christmas. Everyone kept saying that these things happen, but why do they always happen to me?" she said through her tears.

"I'm sorry." His voice quiet, barely audible over the engine with the speed he was driving.

"I don't want your pity!" she yelled and knew he didn't deserve it, but she was tired of people being sorry. It didn't help. Nothing was going to help today.

"It's not pity, Mandy. It's a feeling of helplessness that nothing can help." He was still touching her hair.

Looking up at him, he was driving like a maniac, and she loved him for it. He didn't even know why she was going to Grand Forks, and he was so willing to help. He didn't even like her, but he was helping her. God, she wished he still liked her a little bit. She wished she had just told him about the baby a month ago. Or even before that.

CHAPTER 18

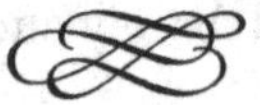

Hue had never driven so fast in his life. But then again, he had never seen Amanda in that much pain. Something was majorly wrong, and she wasn't telling him what. He wasn't going to pry; he knew she would tell him in her time. The timetable of Mandy was something he knew was real. And nobody got in the way.

Stop touching her, he demanded himself and put two hands on the wheel. His heart said to touch her as much as possible while you can. It had been a long month without her, and now he had her again.

Glancing over at her, Hue watched her double over in pain again. It seemed like the same intensity that brought her to her knees on the cold snowy sidewalk in Landstad. The one that scared him to death and was the reason he was driving like a wild man without any indication from her that it was needed. Moving his hand from the steering wheel, he touched her hair, not wanting to hurt her any more than she was already hurting. But she squeezed his hand in a death grip instantly.

Moments later, her grip loosened, and he knew the pain had subsided again. "What's happening, Mandy?" He kept holding her hand but kept the gas pedal pushed to the floor.

"I am having a miscarriage," she said through tears.

"Is it mine?" Gasping, he had to ask, but he knew it wasn't.

Instantly, his mind went to Amanda carrying his baby. Amanda holding his baby, Amanda being the mother to his baby. He wanted it so bad.

"I wish it was. I'm further along than that." She tried to drop his hand, but he kept holding hers. It didn't matter; she was still the woman he loved.

"Does the hospital know you're coming?" They were flying toward it, so he needed to know.

"No," she whispered.

"Do you want me to call?" He got that sense that not enough people knew she was pregnant, realizing possibly nobody knew.

"No, I should." She sat up and pulled her phone from her pocket with her free hand. "How far away are we?"

"I'd say twenty-five minutes if I keep this speed up." He squeezed her hand.

Seeing her dial a number, he expected her to get the emergency room line or even maternity, but he was surprised at how informal she was when the line was picked up. "David. It's me, Amanda."

He could hear the other person talking because of how close they were together in the pickup cab. "Good afternoon, Amanda. How are you?"

"Not good. I'm coming in." There was no panic in her voice. The tears and panic gone completely.

"How far out are you?" The voice turned from friendly to stern and slightly panicked.

"Twenty-five minutes."

"Okay, I'll meet you there. How far along this time?" the voice asked, surprising Hue. They hadn't said anything until that moment about her being pregnant. Not even a hint.

"Thirty weeks on Tuesday," she said calmly.

"Who have you been seeing? Nobody?" David's angry voice got louder as he demanded.

"Nobody." Her eyes were on their still linked hands as she confirmed the other man's suspicion.

"Amanda!" David actually yelled at her.

"There's nothing that can be done," she defended herself calmly to the yelling.

"Of course there is. Fuck, Amanda," the man stated firmly.

"Don't," she said calmly.

"The plan. We will follow the plan." David was quieter now.

"Yes, it won't do any good. But yes," she answered, her voice as sad as Hue had ever heard it.

"I will have everybody ready." It seemed he was already planning.

"Okay." She hung up the phone without saying goodbye.

Hue looked over at her. The tears had stopped during the call but were seeping out again. If his hand hadn't been tightly in her grasp during the call, he would have thought she was as calm as she sounded. But her body was tense, even if she sounded calm.

Glancing at her down-turned face, he asked, "Do you still have to call the hospital?"

She shook her head. "David will."

"Who's David?" he asked, because he couldn't help but wonder if he was the father. Was this guy the father, and were they in love? Had he been just a distraction for Amanda while the guy wasn't around? That he had been a bigger fool than he had thought?

"Dr. David Bennett. I worked with him the last three years I was in Grand Forks, Neonatal Intensive Care Unit. High-risk pregnancies. He was also my doctor for most of my marriage. He's the only one I trust." She was trying to calm her breathing, and he realized she was having another contraction. That was what was causing her intense pain that vanished on its own. Contractions.

When her grip loosened again, he asked, "Who's the father?" Because he had to know. He deserved to know.

"Dr. Paul Masters. I worked with him before I went to David in the NICU. We had been seeing each other on and off for three years. I was stupid." Shifting in her seat, she couldn't meet his eyes.

"Why?" He knew he had to prod her while he had her talking. Even if he really didn't want to hear it, he wanted to know.

"He paid attention to me, and I fell for it. I had just gotten a divorce and was feeling pretty unlovable, and he was charming. I knew he was married, but it felt good to be loved, even if it wasn't real. I had actually broken up with him before I came back to Landstad. I saw the real him, but I went back anyway."

"The speeding tickets?" It clicked in his mind.

"Yes, you were always out there, waiting to give me a ticket when I came back. You gave me a ticket the night I conceived. I broke it off with him completely a week later. I was tired of it. Really tired of it. And for once, it worked." Finally, she looked up and gave him a small smile.

"So, you haven't seen him since summer?" He didn't want to know, but he did. They hadn't even been together then, but he deserved to know when it had ended. Was he a rebound relationship? Was the other man still on her mind?

"No, and he has moved to St Louis since then. He left just before Zia was born. One of the maternity ward nurses told me when I talked to them that day. I used to work closely with them." She had closed her eyes.

"Are you going to tell him?"

"No. It won't matter, anyway. The last baby I lost was his, and he was not upset that it happened. Hence the end of our relationship, or at least the start of the end." Pain overtook her body again, and she squeezed his hand until he could almost feel it breaking.

"I wish you wouldn't talk like it's inevitable that the baby will die. Thirty weeks is viable." He squeezed her hand. He didn't know much about babies, but he knew that.

"Because it doesn't matter. My babies have never come out breathing. David will try, but it won't matter. I was lucky this time. I got Christmas and Thanksgiving with my baby. I have never gotten both before." She touched her stomach delicately.

"Why didn't you tell me?"

"I don't want anyone to know. It's my happiness and pain. I don't need anyone looking at me in pity when it's all over."

"But if you tell people, they will understand what is going on. You realize that while you are dealing with this all alone, your family has been worried sick about you? You may be hiding the reason for the pain, but you're not actually hiding the pain from them." He knew he was lecturing her for no reason, but he couldn't understand how she didn't see it.

"I really tried. It's just how I feel. This is the tenth one, Hue. Ten. And the outcome is always the same."

"Are you going to do the plan?" David had mentioned a plan.

"Yes, and maybe it will work." She looked out the window. Even the way she said the words told him she wasn't convinced it would work at all. That nothing could change what was going to happen.

They were both silent for a few minutes as the scenery rushed by. They were in town now, and though Hue was still speeding, they were going far slower than they had been. It was Sunday, and the traffic was light, but Hue still illegally passed four cars.

"Can I ask what the plan is?" he asked, his eyes on the road.

"C-section. I have always gone naturally. Usually, I am too far gone to stop delivery. If David thinks he can, he will take the baby out," she whispered, and he could tell by her words that it was extreme.

Before he could think too much about the plan, he pulled into the emergency entrance of the hospital. He knew he was blocking the bay doors as he stopped in front of a half dozen men and women already in surgical gear. Jumping out of the pickup, he came around the front as two people were helping her out of the cab. Shaking them off her, she did it herself. Only Amanda would do it herself.

"Amanda Nordskov, onto the bed," a tall man who was covered in thin blue hospital gear said to her sternly.

"Okay." Taking off her jacket as she climbed on the bed, she hunched over. A nurse lifted her shirt as another woman started poking her with needles in the back. The tall man handed her a small plastic cup of something and then started feeling around her stomach. All in the bitter cold, but she didn't shiver or move at all.

Hue squatted down so that his face was even with hers. "Are you okay?"

"No," she whispered. But he knew this was what she wanted despite her words. He leaned over and kissed her lips. They were cold.

It was still fifteen below, and they were working on her outside, but he couldn't stop himself. It was the only way he knew how to comfort her right then, unable to actually touch her in case he got in the way.

"David, are you really having us do this out here?" the woman carefully poking Amanda with a needle asked.

"Yes, I want the epidural in so it can start taking effect—no wasting time getting her to a room." The tall man, who must be David, stated, "Just remember, Sabrina, the faster you are, the quicker you can get inside."

Before the sentence was over, the woman stepped back, and Amanda drank whatever was in the cup, then handed it to the nurse before she rolled onto her back. The moment she was flat on her bed, they finally pushed her into the hospital. Taking her hand as they wheeled her down a hallway, Hue had to nearly run to keep up. At a door, the original group backed off as another group took over. They, too, were fully masked and gowned.

Before he could think, he was pulled away from her hand as a nurse started to help him get a gown on and forced him to wash his hands as she expertly placed a hat and a mask over his face. "Leave the mask on."

When he was fully covered from head to toe, he was sent into the room they had pulled Amanda into. Dr. Bennett was already there and chatting with her, as if there was not a sheet between them. David didn't even look up at him, just changed subjects. "Dad's here. Go hold her hand. I was just telling Amanda that she knew better than not coming in before today."

Hue took Amanda's hand in his. Hers was bare, and his was gloved, but her grip was strong. As he kissed her forehead, he realized that he had a mask on and pulled it down so he could kiss her skin. Her eyes flew to his. "Put your mask on." Pulling the mask back on, he kissed her cheek that was still red from the cold.

A woman sitting by the other side of Amanda's head looked at him, but all he could see was her brown eyes since she was covered completely in person protective clothing, just like he was. She looked down at Amanda and said, "Four minutes." It was only then that he realized it was the same woman from outside, Sabrina. How she had changed so fast, he didn't know.

From behind the wall, David asked, "Do you miss working here? Miss the excitement?"

"Not today. Could use a little less excitement today." She bit her lip hard as a tear rolled down her cheek.

"Five," Sabrina called out from beside him. He didn't know what her count was about.

"Amanda, Grace is here. You remember Grace? She took over your job when you left," David said, but Hue could tell his attention wasn't on the introduction.

"I know. I told you to hire her," Amanda said with a gasp, and Sabrina adjusted something on the monitor by her side.

The door behind them opened and closed, but nobody actually looked at who came in. "Okay, Cruz is here. You know, Mike, right Amanda? He's going to take over with you and Dr. Bennett, and I will go with the baby," Grace explained. "There are no handoffs unless it's an emergency."

"Amanda, this is an emergency," David said. Hue forgot that the curtain was the only thing between them and the doctor, and the doctor was close.

"Six," Sabrina said.

"What are the bones of the hand?" David asked, still too close for Hue's comfort.

"What?" Amanda asked in confusion.

"And point to them. Grace, make sure she's right."

The woman's face became visible to them for the first time.

To Hue's surprise, she actually let go of her tight grip on his hand and started to point at each one and named them. Her hand was shaking a little, but she was scared about what was happening. And happening so quickly.

"Grace?" David asked.

"No shock," Grace said.

"You can stop," David stated.

Instantly, her hand found his again.

"Pretty high, but I can feel that," she said through gritted teeth.

"Does it hurt a lot of or a little?" David asked as Sabrina held Amanda's other hand.

"A lot," she whispered as she bit her lip hard.

Unable to do anything but hold her hand again after the bone count, he leaned down, pulled off his mask, and kissed her forehead.

CHAPTER 19

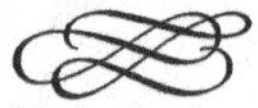

Her blue eyes flew to his, and she whispered, "Put the mask back on."

"Put the mask back on. Twelve." Sabrina didn't say it nearly as nicely as Amanda had.

"Boy. Breathing. Cruz. Grace." By the time the doctor had said the last name, he had to be on the other side of the room.

Grace turned as the doctor walked away and decoded the words for them. "It's a boy, and he is breathing. David has him, and Dad needs to follow me now. Cruz will finish here."

Hue turned to Amanda. They hadn't discussed this. They hadn't discussed anything. He was there for her, though, whatever she wanted. She let his hand go before Grace finished talking and pleaded, "Go with him, Hue. Be with him."

Kissing her lips with his mask on, he turned and quickly followed the nurse out the door. Though she was shorter than him by a nearly a foot, he had a hard time keeping pace with her. Watching her, he realized this had been Amanda until last year. She would have been the one following the doctor as fast as she could. Hue wondered if Amanda missed the fast pace she left behind.

"What was the counting for?" he asked as she started to rip off the plastic gloves she was still wearing. He followed suit, though not as gracefully as her.

"Dr. Bennett wanted a count up from when the epidural was placed. The baby came out during minute six." She stopped at a sink and started to wash her hands and indicated for him to do the same.

"Is that normal? Does it usually happen that fast?" he asked in confusion. He knew nothing about any of this.

"No, just in an emergency. Only twice have I even seen it before." Her hands clean, she pulled a towel to dry them. Looking up at him, she said, "She had to have felt a lot of it. I can't believe she didn't scream."

"She had almost no reaction," he admitted, doing the same.

"She was scared for the baby. That takes over. We checked for shock." She pulled on new gloves with a speed he hadn't seen before. "She knew it was going to happen fast."

"She just said it would be a C-section." He pulled on the new gloves way slower than she had.

"This was the plan. It's in her file. Both knew it without looking at it. I worked under her for three years. She knew everything happening to her, even if David didn't say a word about what he was doing." She chuckled as she said, "Cruz is in there with her, not wanting to touch her for another ten minutes at least."

"Will he?" Hue asked, wondering if she would be in more pain as she waited.

"Yes, he has to." She pushed into the room behind her.

Once in the room, he forgot about the doctor who was sewing up poor Amanda, who was feeling every suture. Suddenly, all he could think about was the tiny infant in front of him. He was small, very small, but he was moving. Not crying, but moving. Another nurse came in, and they continued poking and prodding and pushing tubes into the tiny baby.

"He's doing great. It doesn't look like it, but he's breathing on his own and is a few ounces bigger than I would expect for thirty weeks," David explained, his hands still moving, even if Hue had no idea what he was actually doing.

"Can I have your permission to take a picture to send to my wife when he is stable? Mira worked with Amanda in the NICU before she came up here. Mira was scared when she heard Mandy was being rushed in. Well, we both were."

"Yes, sure." Hue didn't know what to say. It wasn't his baby, but it felt like his baby at that moment. They had already been through hell together, and the kid was only a few minutes old.

David continued to do things to the baby, and a nurse took note of what he was saying. Another nurse gave him everything he asked for before he stopped and looked at Hue. "Can I have you touch him?"

"Me?" Hue looked down at the tiny baby that looked like he would break if he touched him. He wasn't trained to touch a baby this small.

"Amanda will ask if you touched him. To make sure he is real." He knew the doctor was smiling as he explained.

Stepping close to where the doctor and nurses were busy working, he reached out and touched the baby's warm hand. It flexed at his touch, proving he was alive. All he wanted to do was tell Amanda about it, but he stayed with her son. She wanted him to be with her son.

"How is she doing out there in the tundra?" David asked.

"Good. She's liked by everyone in town. I think she likes it." In reality, they never really talked about her job. Yes, she went to work every day, but she never talked about it. Maybe because she was bored with it.

"I wish she was still here. I thought maybe when Paul left, I could get her back. But I don't think I will, especially now." He tapped the baby he was transferring back into a plastic bubble of a crib.

"Yeah, I think everything will change now," Hue agreed. This tiny boy was now Amanda's world.

David was working on the monitors attached to the baby. "Sorry, I'm David Bennett."

"Hue Strong," Hue said to the man who had just saved Amanda's baby. It felt like he had known the man for years. He had done so much for them in less than an hour.

"Oh, I like that." He finished with the monitors. Then he slid out the card that said how long the baby was and that baby it was just under four pounds. David wrote on the top Baby Boy Strong.

Hue was staring at the paper that had just proclaimed the baby was his. It felt right. That baby was his. He loved him as much as his mom. "Hi, little guy," he whispered to the boy who was just staring up at him.

"I guess now all he has to do is live up to his name. He seems to be up for the challenge. Can someone find out if Amanda is in recovery yet?"

A nurse took off to do his bidding.

When word came back that she was indeed in recovery, Hue was shocked he had been away from her for so long. That he hadn't even noticed the time fly as he watched the baby. Since she was in a room, a nurse happily took him there. He hated leaving the baby alone, but he had half a dozen nurses taking care of him. Their hands were far better than his.

Stepping into her room, he thought that she was asleep. Only Mandy would fall asleep within an hour of giving birth. Glancing at his phone, he saw that Math had called, but he put it back in his pocket as he walked up to her bed. There was a more important Nordskov to talk to right then.

Her eyes popped open as he sat down. "How is he? Grace said he looked good. But what do you think?"

"He is little, but Dr. Bennett said he looks really good. He's full of tubes." He took her hand into his.

"Yes, he's thirty weeks," she said like she knew exactly what he looked like in that little bed. Because she did; she had seen it before. "Did you take any pictures?"

"Shoot, no, I was so busy just looking at him. He's amazing, Mandy. Adorable." He kissed her hand.

"Did you touch him?" she whispered to him.

"Yes, I touched his tiny hand. And he wanted to curl it around my finger," he told her in amazement.

Across the room on a table, her phone buzzed. It had been taken here at some point by someone, but Hue had no idea who. Hue went to get it, and since the text was from David, he opened it. As he handed it to her, he said, "David was thinking more clearly than I was."

Watching her page through the pictures of her son, he leaned over close to her so he could see him again. Once they were done, she went back through them. Then again.

"He has your name." She almost touched it on the screen.

"Just for now, you can change it. David thought he needed to be strong today." He kissed her hair above her ear, loving that he could share this moment with her. Wanting to share every moment with her forever.

"I like it," she whispered.

"I do too. I wish he was mine," Hue let slip. Why did he say that? She didn't need to hear that today.

"Me too." She looked at the pictures again, and he wondered if she even knew what she was saying.

Watching her looking through the pictures, he saw that her eyes were free of pain for the first time since the day Zia was born. Today was the first day she wasn't worried about her baby dying at any moment. Finally, she was crying happy tears.

"Do you know any good names? I didn't think I needed one." Giggling, she pulled their hands to her lips and kissed his.

"I can't name your baby, Mandy." He leaned closer to her, needing to be closer to her.

"Grab your chance to name a baby, Hue. Or I will name him Hubert." She smiled up at him.

"God, no. Let's see. I want to name him for you."

"Amanda is a bad name for a baby boy, Hue. Hubert is better than that."

"Math always wanted to name his kid Nordskov Nordskov. You could call him Nordy."

"You and my brother are both bad at this. That's why I always end up naming his kids." She crinkled her nose adorably.

He looked down at her wristband. The way the words were typed on it brought a name to his mind. "Noa."

"Noah? Where did you come up with that one? And so fast after Nordy."

He looked at the picture again. "No for Nordskov, A for Amanda." He touched her wrist band.

"No H at the end?" she questioned, looking at the band herself.

"No need. Noa."

"With an H for Hue. Noah."

"Noah. What middle name?"

"Nordskov."

"So, Noah Nordskov Nordskov. That's as bad as Math's choice." He looked down at her.

"No, Hue. Noah Nordskov Strong. I want him to be yours." She held his gaze.

"I would love him, Mandy. But I don't want you to do something you will regret tomorrow." He hated saying it, but he didn't want her to change her mind and hate it later. Of course, he wanted the baby, but he wanted her to be sure it was what she wanted.

"Just Noah for today then. Tomorrow, we will talk."

"You have to call your family, Mandy." He ran his finger over her wristband again.

"I want to see him first. Make sure this isn't a dream."

"You are stalling, Nordskov," he called her out.

"Of course, I'm stalling. I forgot to tell them I was pregnant. I didn't just forget; I actually hid it from them. For months. They're probably not even home yet." She was looking at the ceiling.

"They are all home. We left over four hours ago. Can you believe that it's not even 3:00 p.m. yet?"

"Yes, I saw how fast you were driving. Thank you for driving that fast."

"I would do it again if you needed it." He leaned down and kissed her. It was the first time he had kissed her since early December, except during delivery, and she tasted the same as he remembered. This was what he had missed the last month. Her. Vowing he would never let her go, he kissed her again.

CHAPTER 20

IT WAS JUST BEFORE 7:00 p.m. when Amanda made it back to her room after seeing her son. She had actually touched her son. She was exhausted, but since she had been exhausted for so long, she wouldn't let it overtake her. With Hue's help, she climbed back into bed. After the covers had been adjusted, she leaned back in the bed and sighed, already missing her son after five minutes away from him.

"Tired?" Hue sat down on the edge of the bed. He was still in the no longer crisp white dress shirt and gray slacks he had worn to the baptism. The tie had vanished long ago, though she was sure he had it on during the delivery.

"Yes. I was up early and had major surgery in the middle of it. I could use a nap." He looked tired too.

"I think you have to call your parents first," Hue pushed her. Now she wished she had just told her parents when she realized she was pregnant. Or after Zia was born. Or when her mom called her fat. Or any other day since she had realized she was going to have a baby. This was going to be hard.

"Are you going to call your mom?" she asked him. At this point, she had no idea where their relationship was. She didn't want to push him in case it scared him off.

"Tomorrow," he said, putting their future back in her hands.

As of now, her future was down the hall, attached to monitors to make sure he was doing everything he was supposed to. When she had finally been able to see him, she had been able to relax a little. Looking over his chart, she knew he was doing better than she had been thinking as she lay in bed recovering. Better than she had ever imagined. But then again, she hadn't imagined he would take one breath, much less an unaided one.

Touching him had been what she had been waiting a lifetime for. To touch her child. Tomorrow, she would get to hold him. Tomorrow, he would be stronger. Tomorrow, he would find out if he had a dad.

She knew she could raise him and could be happy do so alone. But her heart wanted Hue to be there with her.

When she thought about the future, Hue was there.

"What are you doing tonight?" she asked him.

"I don't know. David said I could stay with them, but I don't know them." Every hour or so, David had been back to see them and the baby.

"You'll like them. Mira is great. She's a doctor here as well, but in the ICU. They are a great couple. I delivered their baby," she told him with a smile. It was a few years before, but it was still fresh in her mind.

"I thought you weren't supposed to deliver babies?" he asked in confusion.

She chuckled. "David was so busy proposing to remember she was in labor. She said yes, but after the baby was out."

"I don't see him losing track of what is happening around him," Hue said of the man he barely knew. What little he had seen, it seemed the man was always in control.

"Only when Mira is around." The couple weren't only coworkers but good friends. Over the last year, she had let that relationship slip. She hated that she had let that happen. But for months, every trip she made to town had been to see Paul, and David and Mira didn't like Paul or what she and Paul were doing.

"I think I'm going to run home and come back tonight. Maybe get a hotel room. But I do need some stuff. Do you need anything?"

"Yes, a ton of stuff." She laughed. She had nothing with her, and they had cut off all her clothes. She had nothing but her phone right now.

After making a list, he headed out to get them stuff. He would see her when he got back, but he wasn't waking her if she was sleeping. By the time he walked out the door, she had insisted he stay with David and Mira, and after a text, it was set up. Then he was gone, and she was alone.

She had four hours to make some hard phone calls. It sounded like long enough, but it didn't leave a lot of room for procrastinating. Which was probably for the best since procrastination had gotten her here in the first place.

Picking up her phone, she rang the first number on her list. Mia.

With the phone to her ear, she heard ringing, and she almost hung up when Mia finally picked up. "Mandy, where are you? You're not at your apartment. I have been trying to call, and you don't answer."

"Mia, I can't tell you yet." She hadn't looked at her missed calls or texts before she called. Maybe she should have. She was sure more than Mia was upset with her after leaving the baptism early.

"Mandy, really. I'm not taking that for an answer. I am calling your mom." Mia pulled out the big guns: telling her parents.

"Please don't, Mia. I said it wrong. I need you to get the book club on a conference call in half an hour. Then I will tell you everything—*them* everything." She begged her cousin.

"Okay, I'll try." Mia hesitated as she said it.

"Thank you. I'm calling my mom now. So, you can stop holding that over my head." She hung up on Mia, knowing she was already working on getting the group together on short notice.

And now her mom. Her mom would be crazy mad at her. Forcing herself to hit the button that said mom&dad, she listened to it ring. It was only after one ring that her mom answered the call.

"Amanda Marie Nordskov, where have you been? I have been calling you since you took off during the baptism. During the *baptism*,

Amanda. Math and Tess are furious with you. All you had to do was be there for an hour, and you couldn't even do that. When they asked you to be the godmother, you at least owed them today. I know you let the holidays bring you down, but the holidays are over. It was one day, Amanda." Her mother Dolly berated her. Three "Amandas" in one breath was a feat for even her mom. Especially since her mom hadn't called her Amanda in years. Always just Mandy.

Her mom had wound down and took a breath, so Amanda asked, "Is Dad there?"

"Of course, he is. Where else would he be? It's late." Amanda looked at the clock, but it was only 6:20 p.m.

"Can you put me on speaker phone, so you both can hear?" she asked, and her mom sputtered a little. Her mom hated speaker phone. She listened to her mom talk to herself until she called over her husband to help her, then she got the phone on speaker.

"Okay Mandy, we are here." Her dad's cheerful voice came through. They were on speaker phone. Dad to the rescue.

"I am going to tell you guys something, and I don't want you to get mad," she prefaced, because that had always worked. They couldn't be mad because they were told not to be. Taking a deep breath, she went on. "Today I left the baptism because I was having a miscarriage."

"Not again, Mandy," her mom said, and Mandy could see her face in her mind. She had told the older woman that enough in her life to know exactly what her mom looked like.

"Yes. I didn't tell you that I was pregnant because I knew I would lose him. I didn't want to hurt you again," she explained, hoping it was enough of an explanation.

"But Mandy, it always hurts you more than us. We want to be there for you. We only hurt because you hurt. Well, we hurt too, but you hurt more. Do you want me to come and get you? Will you get out tomorrow morning? I will be there. You should stay here for a little bit, and I will take care of you. Daddy will get you ice cream and pizzas and those candies you like," her mom said firmly, already planning. It hurt Amanda that her mom had a protocol for her miscarriages.

"No, Mom. I won't be out for a few more days. David tried a C-section this time. Recovery is longer; close to a week."

"I will visit right away tomorrow. Or did you want me tonight? I can be there in no time. I will just need time to pack. Dad will drive me in."

Amanda took a calming breath. At least her dad was back to being Dad and no longer daddy. Only when things got rough was he daddy in her mom's vocabulary.

"No, Hue is here with me. You just stay there. But what I want to tell you is that the C-section worked. The baby is alive." She could barely say the words because they still made her cry happy tears.

"What do you mean the baby is alive?" Her dad finally spoke. Her mother must be in too much shock.

"I've touched him. He's little, but he is doing great. Breathing." Mandy couldn't stop the tears.

"Congratulations, Mandy," her dad said, sounding choked up, which made her cry even more because her dad never cried.

"I'm sorry I didn't tell you. I spent a long time just waiting to miscarry. It always happened before. I didn't think this time would be any different," she explained again, hoping the more she said it, the more they would realize she had done it for them. Hidden things to protect them.

"That's why you've been so depressed. You should have told us. We didn't know what to do, Mandy. What to say. Nothing we tried helped this time." She, too, sounded like she was crying.

"I know. I messed up. I'm sorry."

"What's his name?" her dad asked, ignoring what had happened before the birth and focusing on the baby.

"Noah," she said, still loving the name Hue had given him.

"When can we come? Tonight? Dad will be happy to come tonight," her mom asked eagerly. Even if Amanda knew her dad hated driving at night, if she told them they could come, they would.

"Tomorrow. It's late today. But can you wait to tell everyone until tomorrow? I want to make some calls, and I don't want to share him with the world until tomorrow. I want a night."

"Okay, but if you tell Tess, you will have to tell Math," her mom reminded her, knowing that Amanda was closer to her group of friends than she was to her brother, but not by much.

"I will have Hue call him," she said, forgetting her parents didn't know about her and Hue.

Her mom didn't even question why Hue would be the one calling. "Good. And call your sisters—unless you want me to. I would do that for you," her mom said, wanting to tell someone, anyone at this point. Keeping this until morning was going to kill her.

Amanda agreed to let her call Julia and Kit, but not for an hour. And she was sure that by the time that hour was up, she will have called her sister Dottie to rub in a new grandchild. Which would cause Dottie to tell all her girls that she needs more grandchildren. And all this would happen before Hue got back from getting clothes in Landstad.

After she said her goodbyes to her parents, she sent a text to Hue saying that he could call Math and tell him because she was going to tell Tess. And she had told her parents. And her parents were telling everyone soon enough.

Once the text was sent, she waited for her phone to ring. The half an hour mark passed, and no call came in. Maybe she was pushing too much to get everyone on the same phone call. She should have told Mia to get as many as possible on the phone call.

It was just after the forty-five-minute mark when the call finally came in. "Mia?"

"I got them all," Mia said happily. "But we are all at Ruth's, even Tess. Natalie set up some speaker phone thing, so we can all talk. P.S. Tess is pissed at you."

"Tess?" she asked, wondering if Tess could forgive her for what she did. Because she had promised to be there and broke that promise.

"I'm here." Her angry voice came on the line.

"I'm sorry I left today. I did tell you I wasn't feeling very good. I wanted to be there and hated leaving." Amanda knew it wasn't enough.

"I thought you could hold out for a few hours," Tess stated. Not happy, not forgiving.

"I'm sorry. But I had to get to the hospital. I didn't have time to do anything but get there." She waited as the women on the other end whispered amongst themselves.

"Why didn't you come and get me?" Mia's words were quiet, the sadness not hidden. "You said you would tell me. You promised."

"Because I wasn't thinking. Once I realized what it was, I walked home to get my car," Amanda explained, but couldn't because she wasn't thinking at the time.

"Mandy, we were all at the church. You just had to get one of us. And half the people in the church left their keys in their cars. You were in Landstad!" Natalie said, a little louder than she usually talked.

"I didn't want to ruin Zia's day." She took deep breaths to stop the tears that were starting.

"You drove yourself while you were miscarrying a baby?" Mia asked in disbelief, making everyone on the other end gasp because Amanda hadn't told them yet what had happened.

"Baby?" Tess demanded. "What do you mean miscarrying?"

Amanda was relieved Mia seemed to be the one suddenly taking the heat. Though her cousin had done nothing wrong.

"Hey, she swore me to secrecy. Stay mad at her." Mia must be pointing at the phone.

"It's not Mia's fault. She's right; I asked her not to tell anyone. I didn't want anyone to know because I usually miscarry. It's happened far too many times, so I didn't want to share. I wanted to enjoy the baby while I had him. I knew it wouldn't last, and I wanted every day I got. I got Thanksgiving, and I got Christmas and even New Years. I know it seems stupid, but this was my last chance. And I know that Zia's first Christmas was special, but for me, it was his only Christmas. When I had him, he would be gone. So, I held on to every moment I had with him. And that meant not sharing him with anyone." Amanda wiped her eyes on the sheet that covered her.

"You did not say we would need tissues!" Ruth yelled toward the phone. She must have been moving around the apartment.

"Did you really drive yourself, Mandy, alone?" Mia asked, her voice filled with tears.

"No, Hue followed me, picked me up, and drove me. He's been with me the entire time," she said, knowing the others were giving each other looks on the other end of the phone.

"Hue? That's where he went. You both disappeared. I didn't think you left at the same time. So, I didn't think you went together. It makes sense, though. How long has that been going on?" Natalie asked.

"He drove me to the hospital," Amanda stated, not wanting to go into her possible relationship with Hue. Things were to up in the air for that conversation.

"Really? And you got lost on the trail ride the day after Thanksgiving?" Tess demanded.

"It was freezing out that day. What do you think happened?" Amanda blushed at the memory of what had happened on that cold day in the woods. She wasn't going to talk about that either.

"All I know is that you two were forty-five minutes slower than everyone else, and you both looked guilty as sin," Tess said. "Is that when you got pregnant? At my house!"

"No, it was before that." Amanda sighed, and she thought that she heard Tess say something else but couldn't quite make it out.

"So, Hue nicely drove you to the hospital and stayed with you. Is he still with you?" Ruth asked.

"Well, no, he's running home to get us stuff so we can stay here. Neither of us has anything that we need to actually spend any time here. We left so quickly," she explained, hoping that they don't ambush him the moment he gets into town.

"You're staying? For how long?" Mia demanded.

"A few days. I had an emergency C-section," Amanda explained.

"Wait, how far along were you? They wouldn't to a C-section until twenty weeks," Ruth said. She must have been reading her maternity books.

"I was over twenty weeks," Amanda confirmed.

"You mean you were over four months pregnant, and you never

told us?" Natalie said, then added, worried, "I gave you alcohol this morning. Hard alcohol. Did I cause it?"

"No, Natalie. That amount of alcohol wouldn't have done anything. And Mia drank it anyway. She's an amazing friend and cousin," she said, loving how her cousin did everything she could to help Amanda.

"Good, I didn't want to be the cause of this. Me and my stupid new traditions." Natalie sounded defeated.

"It wasn't you. It was always me. I love the new tradition—it was fun. Despite everything that happened after."

"Can we come down tomorrow to visit and try and cheer you up? I think we all feel bad that you are alone during all this. Just when you need someone to cry with," Ruth said, and everyone seemed to agree with her that they would go.

"I am here for a few days because of the C-section, but I don't want you to cry for me." She wiped her eyes again.

"Stop telling us how to feel. For us, this just happened, Amanda!" Tess said angrily.

"I'm sorry. I don't know how to do this. Everything I do I mess up lately." She closed her eyes to concentrate.

"You don't have to say anything. We understand," Hazel said softly. It was the first time she had spoken during the call.

"I wouldn't have called you guys if it had been a miscarriage. I would have kept that to myself. I would have come up with an excuse as to why I left, and nobody would ever know. I called because the doctor saved the baby. He's alive."

"What do you mean, alive?" Natalie said as something fell on their end.

"His name is Noah. I have a son. I can send pictures." Pulling back her phone a little, she forwarded the pictures David had sent earlier in the day, the ones she still couldn't get enough of and had to stop herself from staring at him.

"You better," Hazel said.

"I'm calling Mathias," Tess said at the same time.

"No, Tess. Please. Hue is calling him. He's his friend."

"Okay, but just know we are going to be talking about you later—and Hue," Tess said.

"I know. I'm going to be the talk of the town by morning," she admitted and was happy she was out of town.

"I got the pictures!" Natalie announced.

Everyone went silent as they scrolled through them. There were some oohs and aahs, and Amanda explained why there were so many tubes and monitors. She wanted to look through them again herself just to confirm it was true. It was still hard to believe she had a son.

"Should I point out that his name is Baby Boy Strong?" Mia pointed out.

"I saw that, too. I wasn't going to say anything, but since you did, Mia, I'll ask as well," Ruth stated.

"The doctor put Hue's name on there. He needed to be Strong for a while. But I am thinking about keeping it. Noah Strong," Amanda said the name out loud and still loved it.

"Are you keeping Hue too? Is he yours to keep?" Tess questioned.

"I'm going to try. He might change his mind by tomorrow. Decide it was just adrenalin that had him agreeing to things." She admitted. It was her biggest fear.

"I don't think he'll change his mind. He'll take you and a baby," Mia said.

"I don't know if he wants me," Amanda said.

"Oh, he wants you. Since you dumped him, he's been pretty depressed." Mia was the only one who would know.

"He dumped me," she argued, realizing Mia had walked her right into admitting that.

"Whatever, both of you have been a sight."

"He was already dating," Amanda told them.

"Hardly. He went out with that woman once, and she said he was barely there for that date," Tess explained since it was her who had set them up. "Mathias thought he was lonely. I didn't know anything about you, just that Kit wasn't interested. You could have said something, anything."

Amanda yawned. "No next time. Can you guys just talk about me for a while? I can't keep my eyes open anymore."

As book club said their goodbyes, she was already hovering so close to sleep, she didn't notice their words. Her mind drifted to her son down the hall and the man who wanted to be his dad. Tomorrow, she would have to decide what she wanted to do about them.

Tomorrow would come too quickly, especially if she slept. But she had to sleep; there was nothing she could do to stop it now. The book club ended the call, but Amanda was already sleeping when they did.

CHAPTER 21

HUE CHECKED HIS PHONE AGAIN. Amanda had given him permission to call Math. In fact, she almost said that if he didn't call, Tess would tell him soon, anyway. He checked it one more time to make sure he had read it right, and he had.

The drive was a lot slower going back to Landstad than leaving it today and would take the entire two hours it usually took. It was fully dark now and even colder than before. He was alone in the truck with only the memory of Amanda still in pain.

"Hey, boss, sorry to wake you," Hue said to his boss.

"Good thing you didn't, Hue, since it isn't even 9:00 p.m. yet," Sheriff Sadie Martin said with a chuckle. It was only then that he looked at the time, and though it felt like the middle of the night, it was still early.

"I just wanted to tell you I wouldn't be in to work this next week," he said. He hated to leave the department in a lurch, but he wasn't leaving Amanda's side until he knew she was okay.

"A week? An entire week? You do know that you have to put in more notice than a few hours." Sadie turned all business on him in a heartbeat.

"I'm sorry for the short notice, but Amanda went into early labor today, and I want to be with her," he said, hoping the woman would understand.

"Congratulations, Hue. When did she go into labor? How far along was she? Boy or girl? Is she okay? Is the baby okay?" Sadie asked in rapid fire like she usually did when asking questions. They always seemed to just bubble out of her.

"It's a boy, and they are both fine. Well, both in the hospital, but fine." He shrugged. Did he even know if they were really fine?

"I don't remember you dating anyone, but then again, I probably didn't ask. Well then, stop by the office when you get time. I have some papers you will need to fill out." He could hear her shuffling papers.

"Am I fired? For wanting time off?" he asked in confusion.

"Fired? Why? No, paternity leave. You get six to twelve weeks. But the paperwork has to be filled out," she said. "Oh, and insurance. You'll probably have to take a look at that also."

"I'll fill everything out as soon as possible."

"Good. See you tomorrow."

"I, um, was hoping for time off," he stammered. Was he going to have to tell her again?

"Come in for the paperwork. To fill out the paperwork."

"We're not in Landstad."

"Then I will mail it to you. Would that work? Just take care of mama and baby, and don't worry about us. Oh, but we want pictures. Well, the guys probably don't want them, but I do. I love babies." Her voice was higher than he had ever heard from her before.

"I will soon. Thanks, Sheriff," he said, relieved he had gotten the time off.

"Anytime, Hue." She hung up on him.

Since moving to town, he had grown to respect the woman more and more. Even if she had mostly inherited the job from her father when he passed away, she was capable and competent.

It was after hanging up with her that he had noticed the text and had debated on just letting the man's girlfriend tell him that his best friend and sister had a kid. Or whatever Amanda told her friends.

But thirty years of friendship had him making the call himself. He owed the man that much. Hue hit the button that would connect him to Amanda's brother and his best friend. He had no idea what the man would actually say to him. If he would be mad or happy or a little of both.

"Hue, nice of you to have the balls to call me. After you left the baptism without telling anyone. Before we even ate. I would be pissed at you if my own sister hadn't pulled the same disappearing act," Math laid into him immediately.

"Math. I am sorry. I can explain," Hue said, and knew he was going to.

"Please do. I would like to hear it." He could tell Math had been sure Hue wouldn't call him, probably ever again.

"Is Tess there?" he asked, wondering if the woman had already told Math, and he was just messing with him.

"There was an emergency book club meeting. I hope these don't become normal. She left the baby with me. All I can say is it better not be an overnight thing," Math grumbled, which made Hue smile. Math hated when his woman slept away from him for a night. Hated it.

"I left today because I was following your sister. Who also left?" He was trying to deflect blame, but Math could probably be equally pissed at them both.

"Do not tell me you spent the afternoon in bed with my sister. I do not want to hear about it. And if you tell me you broke her heart again, I will have to pack up my baby and come into town and pound your face in—something I should have done the first time," Math said. Yup, he was a little angry at them both. "Did you at least make up? Did you apologize, so she can get back to normal?"

Math's words made Hue look at the phone in his hand. What did he know? How long had he known?

"I had nothing to apologize for. But that's not the point. I am glad I followed her because she was trying to walk home," he told his friend.

"It was freezing today," Math stated, like Hue had no idea how cold it was out.

"I picked her up before she froze to death," Hue explained.

"I'm starting to think she's gone off her rocker. She's been declining since Zia was born. I don't want to apologize to my sister for having a baby, just because she lost some," Math said.

Taking a deep breath, Hue said, "She is pregnant—*was* pregnant. Since before Zia was born. She has been hiding it from everyone. She did it to protect you guys."

"Are you the dad?" Math asked between his teeth, a little mad.

"No, but I would like to be," Hue admitted and was happy his friend wasn't in the same room as him.

"So, she is no longer pregnant. She lost it again. No wonder she's been so depressed. If she would have said something, we could have helped."

What could they have possibly done?

"I didn't even know until I was taking her to the hospital. She never even hinted." Hue remembered back and didn't up with anything that might have pointed at pregnant.

"Haven't you been sleeping with her?" Math asked, and Hue wondered how he had known.

"Well ..." He didn't know how to answer.

"Come on, you think I didn't notice? Your eyes are always following her around ever since she moved back. Where's Mandy? Just check Hue, where is he looking? Then after the trail ride ..." Math laughed.

"Jerk. You set me up on a date." Hue blushed at the memory and hoped his best friend had no idea what really happened that day.

"I wanted to see if you were serious about her. You passed." Math laughed.

"Thanks," he grumbled.

"Hey, I have to look out for my sisters. They may be independent women, but I don't need them to end up with losers," Math pointed out.

"Thanks," Hue said again.

"Mandy isn't pregnant anymore. I feel bad not knowing." Math sounded saddened by his sister's misery.

"Do you have plans tomorrow?" Hue pushed on.

"No," Math said in confusion.

"Do you want to bring your girlfriend to Grand Forks and meet your nephew?"

"Sure," Math said absently. Then, "What nephew?"

"The baby lived, Math. She was so amazing and brave. She has a baby boy. His name is Noah, and he looks so much like her. Adorable." He bit his lip, trying not to cry about the baby and everything that had happened that day.

"Does Tess know?" Math asked eagerly.

"I think that's what the emergency book club was about. So, Mandy could tell them all at once."

"Did Tess know?" he asked more to himself than Hue.

"I don't think so. I don't think anyone knew. She got pregnant in June, so it had been a long time. She was just waiting to miscarry every day. And just getting more depressed about it every day," Hue explained, which was why she kept getting more and more depressed. Never getting better.

"And you are not the father?" Math asked again.

Hue shook his head, even if he knew Math couldn't see it. "No, but we are talking."

"What does that mean?"

"It means that she asked if I wanted to be the dad. Tomorrow we will talk about it again. I don't want her to make a decision like that when her emotions are running high."

"What happens if you are the dad, but she doesn't want you as a man?" Math asked.

"I don't know. Maybe by tomorrow, I will have figured that out." He wanted the baby, and he wanted Amanda, but did he want the baby without Amanda? Did he really want to be a weekend dad when he wanted Amanda every day? So many questions raced through his mind. But no answers were there.

CHAPTER 22

THEY DIDN'T TALK about it the next day. In the end, they just let it go, and the baby officially became Noah Strong. Neither said yes or no. Neither corrected it. By the time Amanda had woken up, the name was on everything, including the new bracelet on her arm that said his name alongside hers. And a matching one was put on Hue the minute he walked in the door that morning.

Hue was back at the hospital by six and had barely beaten her parents there and hadn't beat her sister Kit, who lived in town. From there was a steady stream of family and friends who came, and by the end of the day, everyone from the book club had been there. Even his mom and sister's family had arrived by evening. All were excited to see Hue's son, and Hue was happy to show him off.

Nobody said anything about the fact that yesterday, most of them had been together, and they had no clue that she was even pregnant. Nobody questioned Hue being there or that his name was listed on the birth certificate. Everybody was just happy to see her tiny baby boy.

There were so many people in and out of the room, she had actually fallen asleep while talking to her sister Julia. When she had woken that time, her aunt and uncle were the only ones in the room, and they were arguing about waking her up.

All day she had tried to get a moment to speak to Hue, but it seemed like she had spoken to everyone she loved except Hue. Hue had spent most of the day in the NICU with Noah, showing people the baby. After all the visitors had finally left, she had crashed and didn't wake until morning.

The following day was no better. Though she had been able to spend the morning with her new son, Hue had to do errands while she did. There seemed to be paperwork he needed to sign at work and so many items that had been forgotten in his initial trip back home. In the afternoon, more people came as word had gotten around town about the birth. Again, she was sleeping before she could say goodbye to him for the night.

Over the next two days, the visitors decreased, but she hadn't been able to talk to Hue alone at all. There had always been someone around, a nurse or a friend. By the time she had been discharged, she was ready to just talk to him. But even then, she found that the few moments where they were alone, they either slept or talked about the baby. Not the future or them, but the baby.

Having worked in the NICU for years, she had never noticed how little time was left for parents to be together, alone. She was able to talk to David more than she was able to talk to Hue these days. They hadn't really talked the month before the baby was born, and now they were still not talking much.

They were treated like a couple, and they seemed to have settled in as a couple. They didn't actually talk about getting back together or about what had torn them apart. Neither talked about anything, just slipped into being a family without working out any of the issues. Issues that needed to be addressed.

Today was Noah's three-week birthday. She had been a mother for three weeks. It was still hard to believe, especially since she didn't have him with her at all times. And never alone away from others. Some days, it felt like others were raising her son instead of her.

She sat on the bed in David and Mira's basement, the place Hue had been staying since the first night, a place she joined him when she was discharged. Since that day, they had been sharing this space, which was little more than a place to crash at the end of a long day. It was the only time they were alone. Not that it mattered; they were too exhausted by the end of each day to do much of anything, even talk. They barely said goodnight before they were sleeping, or maybe it was just her who was exhausted.

Since her body was still bigger than she had been before Noah, she was still in leggings and sweaters. She hated how big she was and saw every extra pound she carried, but there wasn't time to do anything about it. She had more important things to do with her days. But she knew Hue was probably wondering what he had ever saw in her in the first place. She did.

Taking out her phone as she waited on Hue to get done in the shower so they could head to the hospital yet again, she answered texts from family and friends. For the past two weeks, she had been out of the hospital. She was glad they were staying with David and Mira and not at a hotel. Even if she rarely saw the couple, she felt more at home in their house than in a hotel.

The bathroom door opened, and Hue walked into the room, grabbed his socks, and sat on the opposite side of the bed. His focus was on his task when he announced, "Mandy, I'm leaving today."

She didn't see this coming. But looking back on everything, she probably should have. He had no claim to them. It would eventually come down to that they were not a family. That even if he had always wanted kids and a family, this was too much. It was over. Trying to sound like her life wasn't ending, she said, "Okay."

"Math and Tess are coming this afternoon and will bring your car." He grabbed at his shoes, not even looking her way.

"Okay." Unable to say anything else, she just said it again. What else was there to say anyway?

Now she had to plan the rest of her life without him. Except he would always be near, so close but so far from where she wanted him.

"I think Tess wants to take you shopping. For baby stuff." He smiled at her like his words didn't change everything.

Mandy tried to smile back but failed. Tossing her phone on the bed, she went to the bathroom without saying a word. She couldn't. They were trapped behind the lump in her throat. She wasn't going to let him see how much she hurt over this. Because he didn't.

Sitting on the closed toilet lid, she grabbed a towel and covered her face. Letting the towel catch her tears and muffle the sounds of her crying, she stayed there. Trying to recover so he wouldn't see her destroyed.

Hue knocked on the door and asked, "Are you almost ready to go, Mandy?"

Gone was his nickname for her. Gone was the playfulness she had grown to love with him. She should've noticed it was gone, that he was treating her differently. Instead, she had been too focused on her son and had missed all the signs. Again, she hadn't given Hue the attention he needed.

Pulling the towel from her face long enough, she answered, "Just about." But she knew her voice had cracked at the end of the words.

"Mandy, are you okay?" he asked from behind the door.

Again, she lowered the towel and said, "Yes." Maybe it even sounded better this time.

"Mandy?" Hue said again. But this time, he opened the door she hadn't locked. Why hadn't she locked it? "Why are you crying?"

"No reason," she said as he squatted down in front of her.

"Seems like there's a reason." He took her hands in his, letting the towel drop to her lap.

Taking a deep breath, she said the words he needed to hear, the ones that let him off the hook for a mistake he made weeks before. "I understand, Hue. Really, I do. You didn't know what you were getting into here with me and Noah. It's hard. I understand not wanting to do it anymore."

"What are you talking about?" There was confusion in his blue eyes.

Why was he making this so hard?

"You are leaving. I understand." She knew there were tears running down her face. She couldn't stop them, and she didn't try.

"I am not leaving you and Noah, Mandy. I am going back to work tomorrow so that when he is released, I can stay home for a few weeks. I thought I had told you earlier I was planning this. I want to be at home when we bring him home. Help you then. I'm not much help here." His thumb wiped the tears away.

"But I understand if you want to be done with this. It was emotional for a long time. You got swept up in it. I understand if you suddenly see this for what it is. It's a lot."

"And what is it, Nordskov?" His voice was sharp, making her flinch. She wished he didn't call her that in anger only.

"A mistake. I mean, I see what I look like, I understand. You don't want to be saddled with me just because of him." She looked away from his blue eyes staring at her too closely.

"Why can't you ever see you the way I see you? You're the same woman I've been dreaming of getting into bed for over two years now. That hasn't changed. You haven't changed. So, you have a few extra pounds? You had a baby." He pulled her off the toilet seat and onto his lap. His arms went around her, and he held her close.

"I had a few extra pounds then, too," she said into his chest.

"I never noticed that, Mandy. All I see when I look at you is Mandy." He pulled away slightly and kissed her.

Returning his kiss, she realized how much she missed him. Missed his touch, missed his taste, missed him completely. For a long time, she thought that what his touch did to her body was just pregnancy hormones, but to her delight, the feelings were still there. And there were no hormones around. But then again, she thought he was hot when he helped her move into the apartment, and there was no pregnancy then, either. Back then, she had been able to stop thinking of him like that, but not anymore.

As he deepened the kiss, she was a very willing participant. Her hands wandered over the body she had missed touching for so long.

His arms around her were as wonderful as they always were, and his mouth was better than she remembered.

"I missed you," she whispered as his lips left her to nuzzle her neck.

"I was close the entire time." His hand slipped under her shirt and cupped her breasts.

"You were mad." She moaned at the sensations his hands caused.

"Never mad enough that I didn't want you." His hands unclasped her bra so he could grasp the real thing, no barrier.

"I'm breastfeeding," she warned as his hands made her tingle and long for more.

"I know." He rubbed her nipple with his thumb.

Moaning and pushing her breast further into his hands, she said, "They might leak."

He laughed and kissed her exposed neck. "They are."

"This is embarrassing." She blushed and buried her face in his neck.

"No, it's not. It's natural. But we have to stop, anyway." Despite his words, his hands continued their exploration.

"Why?" She nearly moaned the word.

"Because if we don't stop now, I'm going to have a hard time stopping."

"Why are you stopping?"

"Because you can't . . ." He bit her ear instead of saying the last word.

"Yes, I can." She pulled off her shirt and went for his.

"Did your doctor say that?" He slid her bra off her arms and gazed at her breast that he hadn't seen in so long. And if he thought they were big the last time he had seen them, they had grown.

"I don't need my doctor to tell me. I know my body." She shimmied away far enough to start removing his pants.

That seemed to be all he needed to hear. Before she could change her mind, he got off the floor and carried her back into the bedroom they had been sharing for weeks. For that entire time, she had been happy to be able to just sleep with him again. But they were definitely ready to do more. Needing more.

Before they made it to the bed, they had both disposed of the clothes they had recently put on and were naked as they climbed in. Knowing that though not much was said, they had finally talked about them, and there was a them again. Only this time, she was ready to tell the world.

CHAPTER 23

By the time Tess and Math showed up, Amanda and Hue were at the hospital with Noah. For the first time, they arrived at the hospital holding hands and exchanging secretive looks. Or probably not so secretive since not one of the nurses noticed or cared.

After showing the other couple the baby, Tess and Amanda took baby Zia and went out for lunch and shopping, something Amanda hadn't done in the weeks since coming to town. It was good for her to get away since her life had been 24/7 baby since she had him.

With the women gone, Hue didn't know what to do with Math. Usually, his days were spent with his son and Amanda, but Math didn't really want to spend the day looking at the baby. A baby was a baby, and Math had his own. Since they were staying with Amanda's friends, he didn't feel comfortable taking Math there. So, he suggested they go out to eat also.

At the restaurant, they ordered drinks and meals before either really said anything beyond sports and weather. Which, being the end of football season, meant there was quite a bit of sports talk, then add an impending blizzard, and they could go on all day without actually getting personal.

Until it did.

"So, how are things with my sister?" Math asked after taking a long drink of his beer. The man's added emphasis on the words *my sister* were not lost on Hue.

Hue couldn't tell if he was upset or just acting like he was upset. "Good, I think. We don't get much time alone, so we don't talk much. Too much has been happening with the baby." Okay, lame, but he wasn't ever going to tell the man about what happened this morning, no matter how good it was.

"That's how kids are. Get used to it; you won't be able to talk to her for eighteen years. By then, you will be so used to not talking, you won't want to talk, and all she'll want to do is talk." Hue knew for a fact Math was talking about his parents, Dolly and Otto, and it was a perfect summary of their marriage. Then he added, "Are you two together then?"

"That's what we don't talk about. But I think so. I know I am." Hue stated the truth.

"Am I allowed to ask how long you have had the hots for my sister? All these year have you only been friends with me to get to her? How is she not the most maddening know-it-all you have ever known? I mean, really … Mandy? The most exasperating of my sisters?" Math chuckled as their food finally arrive.

Hue ignored his best friend. He knew for a fact that Math loved his sisters and wouldn't trade them for anything. Smiling at the man, he said, "Since she came back."

"But the kid's not yours?" Math hedged as he rearranged his food on his plate, as if the chef hadn't done it right. It was something he had picked up from Tess in the last few months. She did it all the time.

"No, nothing happened for a long time. Because she was your sister, she treated me like a brother, and you should know how she treats her brother."

"Why do you like her?" Math raised an eyebrow in question.

Smiling, he said, "Because she is smart, funny, and cute. I want to spend all my time with her and am always disappointed when I have to leave her. I don't want to leave her."

"That's not what I want to hear."

"And what is it you want to hear?"

"That you love her."

"That I do. So much that when she broke it off, or I did, I didn't know how I was going to survive," Hue agreed. No use hiding it.

"What is Krystal going to say?" Math asked with interest.

"Why would Krystal care? She got rid of me years ago," Hue said of his ex-wife.

"She always hated Mandy. Hated how you two could joke around constantly. That was one of the main reasons she didn't like visiting when my family was around. One of many."

"I never thought about her that way back then. She was married to Seth for most of those years. At the time, I thought they were happy. Hell, I thought I was happy."

"Just saying how it was. So, you never thought of her like that?" Math teased him again.

"No," Hue argued. He had never thought of another woman like then when he was married. Not once.

"High school when she tutored you? Nothing?" Math winked at him.

"Well, I thought she was pretty hot back then, but she was too old and mature for me. Remember how she used to wear those blue glasses all the time back then? How sexy they made her look? And how she would act all cool by wearing sweatpants all the time when I came over. I still have a thing for a woman in sweatpants. Then she went to college, and ..." Hue watched his friend become more and more uncomfortable with each word he said.

"Okay, I will leave it," Math said, putting his hands over his ears.

"Thanks."

"So, are you going to marry her?" Math acted all big brotherly suddenly.

Hue sat back in his chair. "Are you going to marry Tess?"

"Yes, once she says yes."

"I would like to, but I don't know if she does."

"You could ask. I get turned down all the time. It hurts worst the first time, but after that, it gets easier."

"I have to wait until we get the baby out of the hospital and start living a normal life again," Hue told him.

"The more you let Mandy think about things, the more she will twist it all up. Just remember that."

Leaning back in his chair, he looked at his friend, his wise friend. That summed up Amanda perfectly. She was an overthinker. Maybe Math was right, and he should ask her to marry him before he even leaves today. Let her know how he sees her, that he loves her and wants her forever.

When they were done with a long lunch, they went back to the hospital, but Math had to run an errand while his girlfriend was still busy, so Hue went to see his son alone. He didn't get to spend a lot of one-on-one time with his three-week-old.

Scrubbing up, he realized thinking about his son, worrying about his son, didn't get old. The one good thing about the worry was that Amanda had all the answers, and he didn't have to worry unless she did. So, he was happy to let him go without much explanation.

The baby was sleeping when he arrived. Letting him sleep, he looked at the boy, who was naked except for the diaper. His boy hadn't worn clothes yet. He was not as red as he was when he was born, and he was starting to see Amanda in him. Her hair was coming in on his head, and her little button nose was on his face.

"He's doing really well," Dr. David Bennett said from the other side of the crib thing the baby was in. It hadn't taken long for them to become friends.

"That's what Mandy says."

"Amanda would know. How are things going other than that?"

"Good, I think," Hue hedged, because he wasn't 100% sure.

David didn't look up from the baby he was checking. "I understand you're with Amanda. In the beginning, I was questioning it. Neither of you would admit it."

"What does that mean?"

"I worked with her for three years. Mira worked with her for five. Amanda has a thick skin, but she is very tender underneath. She hurts deeply but doesn't let anyone see that." David didn't answer the question at all.

"That is true." He realized the man knew Mandy well.

David only nodded. "I think she could have carried to term if she would have come to see me. Looking back on it now, I think her issue was stress. The entire time she was dealing with the miscarriages, she worked in a high-stress job, not that she ever lets it show. But her body knew. That's why I missed it. But her new job has less stress and fewer adrenalin rushes. I would have put her on bed rest at twenty weeks, and I think she would have carried to term. Next time."

"There won't be a next time, not if she stays with me," Hue told him. It was no secret Noah would be an only child if they stayed together.

"You don't want more?"

Was he holding her back from having more kids? If she stayed with him, Noah was it, but if she married someone else, she could have a few more and have the family she always wanted. Was he being selfish for wanting her? For staying with her?

"I can't. My ex and I went through a lot of tests." He didn't need to elaborate.

"Not with me," David said, as if it mattered.

"No," Hue said, because he would have remembered meeting this man before.

"What's the issue?" David asked.

Shrugging, he said, "I don't really know, just that it was me. She has a kid now."

"Can I run some tests? So that you at least know? It's nice to know the answers." David wrote something in Noah's chart.

"Not that it will do any good, but sure." Hue had taken all the tests before.

"Let me be the judge of that," David said. "I will have a nurse get you what you need."

Before the hour was out, he had been given a cup, and it was done. At least David would tell him what the issue was since the doctors Krystal had seen never would. Maybe it would even be something they could work around. Except he was sure there wouldn't be. Krystal would have used any work-around there was.

When he made it back to the NICU, the baby was awake, and the nurse helped him hold his son. Usually, he let Amanda spend as much time holding the baby as she could take, which was a lot of time. So, he enjoyed his time with the infant before he went to work for a few weeks. He would be back often, but he would miss the everyday of it here. But he knew he was going to love spending a few weeks alone with Amanda and his son. It was worth missing out now for then.

CHAPTER 24

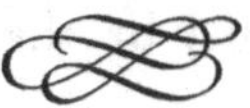

SITTING DOWN ACROSS FROM TESS, Amanda looked over at the baby in her car seat. She was almost three months old now. Amanda could see Noah looking like all of her nieces and nephews. Including this one.

Tess caught her looking. "Do you feel better about babies now, or does she still bother you?"

"No, I am better now." Amanda turned to her friend. "I am so sorry for how I was when she was born. I was awful—to you and to her. I could tell you that I tried hard to be better, but I failed miserably."

"Mandy, I understand now. If you would have just told me. Not knowing made it feel like you weren't happy for us. About her. I thought that I had lost one of my closest friends, all because I accidentally got pregnant."

"I thought I had to be alone with my misery, my joy." Amanda half smiled.

"Mandy, I am your friend, and I hope your family. I want you to know I am there for you for every joy and misery in your life. I am always there. But so is everyone from book club."

"It's just hard letting others in," she admitted. "I have missed book club. I'll be ready this weekend. I've been listening to the book. I'm hoping nobody in the NICU can hear what I'm listening to." Amanda laughed. It was Richard Ramirez this week. Not a baby-approved topic at all.

"You have been forgiven. But it was not a unanimous vote," Tess told her, but Amanda was sure Tess was a nay vote.

"I can't wait to get home. I love David and Mira, but I'm tired of being a houseguest," Amanda admitted.

"What's your plan for when you get home? Stay uptown or move?" Tess asked. She lived out on her brother's farm but had lived downtown for over a year.

"I don't know. We haven't talked about it. I will definitely stay where I am for a while and see what happens then."

"Maybe Ruth has a two-bedroom available?" Tess said of their friend who owned most of the downtown buildings. Though she always seemed to keep them full somehow.

"I will have to talk to her. How is she doing?" Amanda had missed Ruth's latest appointment and was feeling bad about it. She hoped that by the time she had her next, she would be back. But then she remembered she wouldn't be working for another month or so.

"I've not heard anything about her not being okay. Don't worry about her; she knows you're busy."

"I'll give her a call one day." Amanda made a mental note she would hopefully remember. Lately, mental notes were the first ones she lost.

"How much longer will you be here?" Tess asked.

"Another three weeks if there are no complications, but he has been perfect so far, so I don't see any issues," Amanda said as their food was dropped off.

"Perfect, huh? Is that the nurse or the mom talking?" Tess started to cut her chicken sandwich into tiny pieces.

Laughing at her friend both for her odd eating habits and for her comment, she answered, "Both, thankfully."

"He looked perfect, though not much like Zia," Tess admitted.

"He's getting there. I can see it, but I'm used to premies. By Zia's first birthday, you'll not be able to tell them apart." Amanda looked over at her niece, who was awake and looking around. Reaching over, she picked up the baby for almost the first time since she was born. The girl was heavy compared to her cousin and Amanda analyzed her face. She was definitely her brother's baby.

"Her eyes are turning," Tess said from across the table, her gray eyes looking at her baby.

"How did you get a gene into a Nordskov?" Amanda demanded.

"I have some pretty powerful genes, too." Tess grinned.

"Can you imagine a Nordskov with gray eyes?" Amanda hugged the baby to her.

"I am thinking she won't be the only one forever," Tess said as she ate her chicken.

"Are you having another one?" Amanda demanded, loving the idea of her brother with five kids, maybe six.

"No, no babies. I'm thinking of changing my name." Tess smiled at her answer, because all she had to do was say yes to Math, and they would be married in a heartbeat. The man was dying to marry her.

"Really? Why? I mean, you've never been too keen on the idea," Amanda said. Tess had said no so many times over the last few months—what changed?

"It's time. I want to share her name. Mathias's name. Mathias's life."

"You can get married and keep your name."

"I could, but I want to change it. I want to share my husband's name. Belong to him."

"I want you to change it, too," Mandy said. "Does my brother know?"

"No. I'm going to ask him this weekend. He's asked me so many times I don't think he would believe me if I said yes. But if I asked, he will know I want to marry him."

"He will be so excited," Mandy said.

"I think so."

"So, how is the town taking the baby news?" she asked.

"Okay, I think. I haven't heard too much. But then again, I'm not someone everybody gossips with. Mia has been deflecting a lot, though," Tess said about her cousin.

"I will have to thank her."

As their conversation turned to local gossip, Amanda let her mind slip back to the bedroom she and Hue shared and wondered what it was going to be like when he was gone. As of right now, it looked like Noah would be spending another three weeks in the hospital. So, three weeks before he would be with her full time—both of her boys.

As they paid their bill, Amanda followed Tess around the rest of the afternoon, picking out things she would not use for another three weeks or more. Realizing as they had a cart full of stuff, all she wanted was her baby and Hue and to be home. Then she could think about all the stuff they would need to make Noah happy.

Hugging Tess goodbye at the hospital when Math came to pick her up, Amanda knew she had missed her friend these last few months. Now that her emotions were more on an even keel, she could get back to having friends. Back to just being with people. Back to being herself.

As she approached the NICU, she saw Hue through the window and just stopped and watched him. He was sitting in a chair shirtless, holding the baby on his chest. If she had ever doubted that Hue loved the baby, she forgot it now. Noah was as much his as he was hers, she could see that. Hue saw her in the window and waved at her, so she smiled and waved back. Quickly, she went to get washed up to see her son and his father.

CHAPTER 25

FEBRUARY WAS ALMOST over before David released Noah from the hospital. It was just over seven weeks from his birth when he was finally allowed to go home. That Tuesday morning, he headed out bright and early to bring his family home, and Hue had started his three-week leave. Driving down as the sun came up, he brought the car seat and a few other things that might be needed for the drive back with their son, but he really had no idea what was needed.

When he got there, the nurses were showing Amanda everything that was needed to keep the little boy alive. Hue would have been terrified about bringing him home if he didn't have Amanda at his side. With Noah in her arms, he knew she was barely listening as the instructions were told to them, but she used to give the instructions, so she didn't have to listen.

Over the past month, he had spent every weekend with her and usually two nights a week, always getting up before dawn to get to work on time. But it had all been worth it to spend time with Amanda and Noah.

Since the day he went back to work, when they were alone, they couldn't keep their hands off each other. The only downside was that they were still guests at David and Mira's house; though they were great people, and Hue got along with them, he wanted his family home.

But where was home? They hadn't discussed it, but they couldn't stay downtown forever. They each had a one-bedroom rental. Neither was big enough for all the stuff Amanda and Tess had already bought, much less what was bound to show up when they finally got back to Landstad. But he didn't push Amanda on the living situation when her sole purpose was on getting Noah out of the hospital. When she got back to Landstad, she would instantly be aware of what the issue was.

"Did you get him all in there?" David asked as he looked at the baby in the car seat that was far too big for such a little boy.

"Yes, we did, and he's pretty excited to see his home," Amanda said about the baby who didn't seem exactly excited. Very mad was how Hue would describe him. But Hue didn't know babies like Amanda did.

"I bet he is. You have everything you need?" David asked them both, but mostly Amanda because she knew what they needed.

"I have Mandy, so yes." Hue touched the woman on the arm, making David laugh.

"I would take her over anything else in this place too." David winked at Amanda, who just took the compliments and readjusted the baby one more time.

"So, can we just take him? No alarms or anything will go off?" Amanda asked.

"Nope. But I do want to talk to your … Hue. A moment." David pointed at him.

"You may speak to my Hue for a moment, but I want him back." Amanda laughed at the doctor's stumble.

As they walked away, Amanda started to look through the bag on the floor next to her again. David led him into the hallway, and Hue was able to see Amanda through the big window that separated the two. She didn't notice him. Hue stopped when David did and was wondering what he could possibly have to say to him that he couldn't say to Amanda. Maybe it was the 'make an honest woman out of her' talk, which made him wonder how close the couple was with Amanda after all.

"So, Hue, can I ask again how much infertility you went through? Before."

David's question took him by surprise. It had been weeks since they had talked about this. Maybe his infertility was something more serious than Krystal ever let on.

"About six years." Hue tried to remember, but he didn't know exactly since his ex didn't make the process a couple's thing. Mostly, she didn't talk about it at all. She was far more embarrassed about it than she should have been.

"What kind?" David inquired.

"Shots, pills, I don't remember what it all was." He told the truth.

"Did you see a doctor?"

"Well, once, but my wife—ex-wife—was always the one talking to the doctors." Hue didn't need to be told of his failings more than once. Krystal had told him all the time.

"Because I ran some tests, and I don't see anything wrong with you. Everything looks good. There is no reason that you shouldn't be able to father children if you want." The doctor just shrugged.

"No, David, I can't father children. She has a baby. I don't."

Amanda stood up and looked at him, then smiled and waved from inside the room. The baby must have made a noise because she was back down with him in an instant.

"I don't know what to tell you. Medically, I can't find anything wrong. So, when you and Amanda start to get intimate, you should be using protection." David slapped him on the back after Hue looked back at the woman who had insisted she was ready last month. It seemed that she and her doctor were not on the same page if he didn't know they were already intimate. "If you decide to have more kids, she sees me constantly the moment she even thinks about getting pregnant."

Leaning against the wall, Hue had no idea what to think. As David's phone rang, he looked at it and walked away quickly with a small wave, leaving Hue alone with his thoughts. Maybe the tests he took now were wrong. They had to be wrong. Because the ones he took ten years before couldn't be wrong. Except all evidence said they were.

A few minutes later, when Amanda came out, he was still leaning against the wall, still in shock. David had to be wrong. He had known for years that the problem was with him. Krystal had said so. She had a kid. If it had been her, how did she get a kid?

Looking into her smiling face as she carried the baby toward him, he wondered how he was going to tell her. What if she was pregnant again already? Suddenly, it was him who would be the one who put the baby in her that she would miscarry. He would be the cause of her pain.

Pulling her to him, he kissed away the pain he could possibly cause her in the future. Knowing he would be by her side through the entire thing didn't ease his worry. Because she could leave him easily enough. He had no hold on her.

She pulled away from him and handed him the bag she had slung over her shoulder. "Let's go home, Hue."

Turning, he took her hand with a smile and led her from the hospital they had almost called home for two months. It was the same route they had taken the night Zia had been born. But this time, they were leaving with their son, their family.

Noah must have known he was leaving the only home he had ever known because he cried the entire drive. Two hours of steady crying from the back seat. Nothing they tried worked to stop it. By the time they reached the apartment, both adults had gone a little crazy.

Amanda spent the next hour just getting him settled down, fed, and put to sleep. Hue felt useless. A few hours later, when the baby woke up a bit more even-keeled again, Amanda fed him, changed him, and just held him for a while until he fell back to sleep. Hue felt useless.

So, it went for the first five days they were home. Amanda did everything. Hue did nothing. Every time he asked if he could help, she said no. He might as well have stayed working. At least there, he was useful.

On the afternoon of the fifth day, it was book club night. Hue said he could watch the baby since Amanda would only be across the street. And didn't she need a night away from the baby? He knew he could handle a few hours with their son. He was capable of that. But Amanda had insisted she had to take him to show the girls. All of which had been through the apartment over the course of the four previous days. He didn't argue. It was no use.

So, Hue had nothing to do all afternoon. Football season was now over, and there was only basketball, which held no interest to him. All he had to keep him company was his thoughts. And they were not comforting.

Pulling out his phone, he called Math. His friend was probably home alone with his kid, because his girlfriend trusted him. "Hey, Math, it's Hue."

"Hey Hue. Are you on baby duty too?" Math rubbed it in.

"No, I don't think she trusts me." He admitted the truth.

"I wouldn't either." Math chuckled.

"Thanks." He felt even worse. His friend didn't even think he could take care of his son.

"I'm kidding, Hue. Tess didn't trust me with the baby either, and I had three before. Three, and she hadn't had one until Zia came. But who was the expert? I will tell you, her. Not to mention you're actually dealing with a baby expert over there. An actual expert. Give it time. She'll relax," Math said, calming his anxiety just a fraction. Then he added, "Or not, she is Mandy. If you only would have talked to me before having a kid with her, I would have told you that. But no, you had to do that all behind my back."

Ignoring the bard, Hue sighed. He was happy Math and everyone else were accepting him as Noah's dad. Only family and the book club even knew Hue wasn't the actual dad. Though he didn't see how people thought that he and Amanda had been together for months without anyone finding out.

Shaking his head, he admitted, "I just feel worthless all the time. She does everything for Noah, and I can barely even hold him some days."

"I know, it will pass. She's still looking at him as a miracle and trying to get all her moments with him."

"I do too. I want my moments," Hue admitted.

"You will get your moments. You will get to teach him to throw a football. No way my sister is ever doing that. And you can teach him to play video games. Another thing Mandy can't master." All of it true, but it didn't help him when the baby couldn't even hold his head up yet.

"You do know one day I will tell her all the stuff you say about her to me, and she will remind you how well she can throw a punch." Hue smiled at all the times he had watch the oldest Nordskov get the better of her little brother. He always deserved it.

Math laughed. "She is a mom now. She wouldn't do that. But seriously, just talk to Mandy. She'll understand."

"Maybe, I don't know." Talking to Mandy when she didn't want to talk never worked.

"She will," Math assured him.

After hanging up with Math, Hue couldn't decide if he felt better or worse. But no matter how he felt, he needed to talk to Amanda about this. Before, it had led to a fight. One he would regret as much as the fight over his mom's health. Probably more, because now he knew what it was like to be without her, and he never wanted to do that again.

After staring at his phone for a few minutes, he placed another call, one he had been thinking about making since they got home. One he didn't want to make. Not ever. But one that needed to be made before he talked to Mandy.

"Krystal, it's Hue."

"Hi, Hue. How are you doing?" The woman sounded bored, the same way she talked to him for the last three years of their marriage.

"Fine." He wasn't going into everything great happening in his life. She wouldn't even want to hear about it. If it didn't involve her, she wasn't interested.

"Oh, fine, is it? That's not what I heard. I heard you're dating Math's big frumpy sister. Not even one of the pretty ones. I know the pickings are limited in Landstad, but couldn't you do better than that?" His ex seemed to be in a bad mood today. Hue was happy he didn't have to live with her anymore. Maybe it was good his marriage had broken down.

"Krystal, I'm not talking about Mandy with you," he stated sternly, realizing she had always been like this. He had just ignored it, but not anymore.

"You know, I saw it coming. You two were constantly flirting with each other. Always. I couldn't stand her. I don't know how Seth put up with her for so long," Krystal admitted.

"Well, I think the feeling was mutual," Hue said under his breath and leaned back on the couch.

"She thinks she's so great because she's a nurse. Just a nurse." Krystal's back was up. Her attempt at college had lasted a year and had just put them into debt for nothing.

"Stop it, Krystal. I want to talk to you for a moment. Do you know what was wrong with me during the fertility stuff?" Hue asked, rubbing his eyes with his fingers, hating talking to her about this. She had always been defensive about the issue.

Krystal huffed into the phone. "I don't remember, Hue. But I would definitely check that baby she is claiming is yours. Because it's not."

"Do you have any records or something that might say?" he asked, trying to get her back on task.

"I don't keep things about you. I'm married to someone else. Someone without so many issues and weird friends." She didn't let up for a moment.

"Did you have to go through fertility treatments for your baby?"

"Of course, Hue. But I was not the problem. That was always you."

Hue hung up on her, tired of talking to her. How had he been married to her for so long?

What she told him said everything. It was her. If it had been him, she wouldn't have had to go through fertility treatments with the new guy. She had lied and said it was him for years. And he had just bought it, trusting his wife would tell him the truth.

And now he had to tell Amanda that not only had his wife lied to him, but that he had believed it without ever checking. And they had been having unprotected sex for a month now. Would the news send her into a depression? Was Noah enough to keep her from that?

When was he going to tell her? How was he going to tell her?

Now suddenly, he was the one who didn't want to talk.

CHAPTER 26

AMANDA SAT STARING at the two lines in front of her. What did it mean? Well, she knew what it meant. It meant she was pregnant. But how was she pregnant? Well, she knew how it happened. She could even tell you how good it was when it happened. Though a date wasn't so readily available, it was always good.

What she didn't know was how it happened? How she was pregnant? The only man she had been with was Hue, and Hue couldn't get her pregnant.

Maybe it was residual hormones that tricked the test. Noah was two months old now, but maybe the residual could still be there. It made perfect sense—if she didn't already know she was grasping at straws that didn't exist.

She threw the test in the trash and covered it with a dozen tissues, then added a dozen more for good measure. There was no way she was pregnant. She had only taken the test because she felt queasy two mornings in a row. Her period had not shown up, but she had a baby not that long ago. It happens.

Hue was never going to believe she was having his baby. Never. But how long could she hide it? Maybe she could sneak away one day and get tested at the clinic. Since she had been gone, there had been another nurse practitioner working there. Or maybe she should go see David.

But Hue was off for almost another two weeks still. She wanted to know before that. And she wanted to know for sure before she told Hue. Because if she told him, and he believed it was true and it ended up not being true, he would be devastated. So, she had to hide it for a bit.

And, of course, today was a Tuesday. A dreaded Tuesday. Always a Tuesday. She really couldn't think on Tuesdays.

Getting up from the toilet seat she had been sitting on, she calmly brushed her teeth. A normal, everyday thing to do for a woman who had a two-month-old baby … and was pregnant with her lover's baby, a lover who couldn't have children. Dropping the toothbrush in the sink, she rushed to the toilet and threw up. Three days in a row now.

When she was done, she sat on the floor, leaning against the wall, head back, eyes closed. What was she going to do? This was as bad as the last time. And see how that turned out. Okay, okay, she ended that one with a baby and a lover, but could she get that again in the end? Not a chance.

She needed to call someone, anyone. Well, not anyone. Her mom was not getting the call. But who? It was midmorning on a Tuesday, so who wasn't working? Everyone was working! She knew she could call any of them, and they would be here in an instant, but Hue was here. It was hard to hide this from Hue when everyone was there talking about it.

Okay. Plan, Amanda, she demanded of herself. *Plan.* Ruth had her appointments on Tuesday. Maybe Ruth didn't want to see the new guy, she wanted to see Amanda. That might work. But no, she couldn't go to the clinic and see Ruth; she needed to see Ruth in her office. Ruth's office across the road. Ruth went to David now, but she wanted to talk to me in person. Plan set.

Scrambling off the floor, Amanda quickly brushed her teeth and washed her face. Out in the main room of her apartment, Hue was watching TV, holding their sleeping son. Perfect. Not just the adorableness of the two, but that Hue was busy, and baby was sleeping.

"I just got a call from Ruth. She wants to talk to me. Do you think you can watch the baby for a few minutes?" she said in a rush as she walked across the apartment, trying to act perfectly normal. "Of course, you can watch him, you're his dad. Can I go?"

Hue looked over at her in confusion. "Sure."

"Thanks." She headed for the door. He bought it!

"Nordskov?" Hue questioned her, and her heart soared at the nickname. It was back. Just in time for this.

Stopping, she turned, trying not to look panicked. "What?"

"Are you going in that?" He pointed at her outfit.

She looked down at her pink lounge pants and white T-shirt. She couldn't care about her outfit when she was in crisis. "Um, yes. I won't be long. Call if you need me."

Once out of the apartment, she bound out the door and was almost across the street when she realized she had not put on a jacket or actual shoes. Her slippers were caked in wet, dirty snow, AKA snirt. But she made it to Ruth's office door and pushed the door open. Or tried to since it was locked.

What now? Mia was at the restaurant full of people. Tess was at the bank, but it was two blocks away, and her slippers would never make that. Natalie and Hazel were both at the high school, which was even farther than the bank.

Reluctantly, she turned to go back home. She would have to deal with this herself. So much for always being there for her. Promises broken.

"Mandy? Is that you?" Ruth asked as she crossed the street, her feet incased in black knee-high boots, perfect for the conditions.

How bad must she look if she wasn't even recognizable? And she was on Main Street! "Yes, Ruth, it is me! I need to talk to you. To someone. Please."

Ruth walked past her and unlocked the office door as slowly as humanly possible. Amanda looked up to her apartment window to see if Hue was looking out, but she didn't see him. Thank god!

Ruth had worked in the same office since high school, only recently moving from being a personal assistant of her now boyfriend, Anderson, to running her own rental office. As the owner of half the buildings on Main Street, she had a lot of rental property. But what mostly kept her busy was her true profession: writing romance novels.

Once Ruth was inside, Amanda pushed past her and grabbed the door out of her hand and pushed it shut again. Locking it, she pushed her friend into the inner office where Ruth did her writing, and nobody was actually allowed. She always came out to her old desk to talk. Once in the inner office, Amanda locked that door also. Why? Since nobody could get past the first door, anyway. But she did it.

Turning while leaning against the door, she looked at her friend, who was still in her white winter jacket. Then she shook her head and took it off. Amanda saw that she was way more pregnant than she had been before Noah was born. Though she had seen the woman in the last week, she hadn't noticed how big she was until now.

"Wow, you're really showing," Amanda said, her eyes not leaving the woman's midsection.

"Is that the reason for this visit? To tell me I'm fat?" Ruth sat down in her desk chair, arms crossed.

"No, of course not. Just saying. You are pregnant. I am fat. There is a big difference." Amanda was still leaning against the door.

"Then why are you here?"

"You are the only one who doesn't work. Well, you work, but you can have visitors." Mandy kicked off her slippers that had snow melting off them. In her bare feet, the floor was freezing cold.

"You are just full of nice comments today." Ruth sounded weary.

"I need help, Ruth. I need so much help." Mandy let her head fall in defeat.

Perking up, Ruth said, "And you came to me with your problems. You chose me to confide in? What can I help you with?"

"This is so much worse than the whole Noah thing," Amanda whispered, admitting it for the first time.

"Nothing is worse than that." Ruth pulled out her phone and started to type. "I will see if anyone is available. Those uptown, at least."

"I need help," Amanda said again, staying leaning against the door.

"I am just happy you are willingly admitting it, Mandy. Now sit down, and I will unlock Fort Knox here." Ruth got up and headed for the door.

In retreat, Mandy rushed to a chair on the other side of Ruth's desk and sat. She wondered why it was there if nobody was allowed in the office. What was the point of the chair? And the one right next to it? Were they for sex? Hot office sex in uncomfortable chairs?

When Ruth had unlocked the door and went to unlock the outer door, Mandy put her head between her knees since now her head was spinning. She should not have come here. Of course, she was smart enough to get out of this by herself. She had done it before, and that almost worked out okay.

Before she lifted her head, she heard Mia rush in. Of course, Mia was across the street and two buildings down at the café. Mia was her favorite cousin; she would be able to figure this out.

Hearing Ruth close the door to the inner office, she sat up, but her head spun again, and she had to hold it. Ruth was there, as was Mia, and even Tess had made it in no time. All three were looking at her in concern.

"Okay, Mandy, spill. What do you need help with?" Mia sat on the corner of the desk.

"I have no idea what I should do." She hoped she wasn't crying, because she couldn't tell right then.

"Well, we can't help unless we know what your choices are," Tess said from the formerly empty sex chair. She had moved it closer to Amanda's own sex chair. Could they both be sex chairs? How kinky was that?

"Okay." She took a few deep breaths and tried to forget about the sex chairs completely. "So, I don't know if you all know that Hue can't have kids. His ex and he went through the whole fertility thing a few years ago. So, he knows he can't. Tested and failed. He doesn't say how it all doesn't work, but it doesn't work."

"I knew that," Mia said, assuring the group she had the knowledge.

"And I haven't been with anyone else since Noah was born. Or before that too, but that doesn't matter. Heck, the last guy I was with was when he was conceived. Noah, that is. Not Hue." Knowing she was rambling and stopping were two different things.

"Well, now we do," Ruth said from her desk chair.

Turning, she glared at Ruth for a moment, then looked at Mia for a moment and Tess, who looked uncomfortable in the other sex chair. "I think they have sex in the chairs. Why else are the in here?"

Tess started to laugh at her. She knew it was at her and not with her because Amanda wasn't laughing. Mia was laughing also.

"Are you on something?" Ruth demanded

"No, I think I'm having a mental break because I think I'm pregnant." Amanda quickly covered her face with her hands.

"But your baby is little," Mia gasped, pointing out the obvious.

"Yup, I know that." Amanda glared at her between her splayed fingers.

"So, you don't want a baby with Hue?" Ruth looked at her in confusion, probably wondering how she cracked the code of the sex chairs.

"Of course, I want a baby with Hue, but he can't have a baby, and I shouldn't have a baby again yet. It's too early for that again, right? They will be like six months apart. Seven? Eight? Why is math so hard?" She groaned.

"I don't see the issue. Just talk to him. All it takes is one good swimmer." Mia made a hand gesture that more resembled a snake to Amanda. "Or maybe his swimmers were all killed by Krystal. I can understand her uterus being uninhabitable."

"I'm glad I never met this woman." Tess ran a hand over Amanda's hair in comfort.

"I took a home test. It was positive, but I only had one. And it was over a year old. I don't know if that's considered old with pregnancy tests. I would assume not. Anyway, I can't go down to the clinic or even to Grand Forks or I have to tell Hue why I'm leaving because he's home for two more weeks. I don't want to tell him if I'm not really pregnant, but I can't get away to even get tested." She dropped her hands and looked at the ceiling.

"What about your miscarriage issue?" Tess asked and took Amanda's hand in hers.

"I don't know. David said it might have been stress and that we would monitor it very closely if I get pregnant again. But I'm not too worried. I guess I am more excited to have Hue's baby than worried I will lose it. I mean, if I do, I still have Noah at home," Amanda said to the ceiling.

"So, you want to confirm it before you tell him, just in case. But what if he accuses you of cheating since he is not supposed to be able to knock you up?" Ruth asked.

"I don't know. It's possible. I don't know where I would have found someone to cheat with. Would I have gone to a bar and picked up someone? What do I say, 'Oh, don't mind the giant wound on my stomach and that my boobs are leaking? Let's have sex.'" Maybe she should learn to keep her mouth shut.

"I have about four pregnancy tests upstairs if you want to try some more. There are different brands. And all newer than yours." Ruth looked above her to where her apartment was.

"Let's." Mia jumped off the table.

"Everybody upstairs." Tess ushered everyone out of the office.

Amanda slid on her soaking wet slippers and went with the group up to Ruth's apartment. Ruth left her in the bathroom with the small group of tests sitting on the counter.

Within half an hour, they were all looking at four tests that said the same thing. Amanda was going to have two babies in one year.

"See, I told you," she whispered at them.

"I do," Tess said from beside her, looking and not touching the one in front of her.

"I've never seen a positive one before," Mia said from her other side. "Let's hope this is it for me for a while. No need to see too many positive pregnancy tests too often for us single ladies." She looked around the room and scrunched up her nose. "Or me, the single lady."

"If anyone tells Anderson I let you put those on the table, all of you die," Ruth said from across the table.

"So, if they are 95% accurate, and you took five, what is the possibility that you are not pregnant?" Tess asked.

"I hate math, and I know that number is very small." Mia got up.

"I love math," Tess said with a laugh. "I also love Math."

"Very cute. Inappropriate, but cute," Amanda said, still looking at the tests.

"I thought so. And not to take anything away from Mandy and whatever this is, but I got engaged yesterday." Tess held up her hand and showed off her sparkling diamond.

"Really, Tess, you could have waited until my crisis is over."

"Your crises never end. You just have to tell him. If he doesn't believe you, Math will kill him. Now that we are engaged, I can tell him to do anything. It's a known fact." Tess laughed as the other two looked at her ring.

Mia looked away from the ring to Amanda. "My god, you two. Between you both, I will never get Mom off my back. Math had a baby and is engaged, Mandy had two kids in one year. Two! How am I going to compete with that? There is no way I can compete with that." She laid her head on the table, careful to avoid the pregnancy tests.

Ruth grabbed a garbage can and went to the table for the pregnancy tests. "Tess is right; don't drag it around with you forever. You'll keep putting it off. Remember how you do that? Or do I have to introduce you to your son."

"Fine, I will go do it, but I think I need to borrow some shoes. I don't think those will make it across the street." She pointed at her once comfy slippers. They were a total loss.

"You can borrow my shoes, but only if you're going to tell him." Ruth went into her bedroom to get her some shoes.

"Everyone says yes, so I'm doing it." She tried to fake a smile but failed. What an emotional day. "But on the plus side, if he stays, I will get a few months of pregnancy hormone sex. I kind of miss it."

"It's a nice side effect," Ruth agreed with her.

"I miss it too," Tess complained.

Mia's head finally came off the table. "Really? Pregnancy sex and a guy to go with it. You guys get everything."

CHAPTER 27

IT HAD BEEN over an hour since Amanda had rushed out of the apartment, leaving Hue alone with the baby for the first time ever. And he was killing it. The baby was sleeping and had a new diaper on.

Unfortunately, when he woke up, he would be starving, and that was one thing Hue didn't have. Food. He would just have to call her then and admit defeat. But until then, he was killing it.

Part of him wondered what was so important at Ruth's to have her leave in her pajamas, but the other part of him was happy she trusted him with the baby. No matter what she wore to visit her friends. Laying the boy in his crib that was currently in the dining room, he looked around at the stuffed-full apartment. One-bedroom apartments were not made for two people and a baby.

Today, he would have to bring up the subject of finding a place together—a bigger place. So far, he had put it off so that she could settle in, but she should be settled in by now. With all the baby stuff, he still had all his stuff in his apartment—there wasn't even room for his clothes.

Once they had that conversation, they had to talk about what David had told him. And that he had basically confirmed with his ex-wife that he could have kids. Though he didn't a 100% believe them, maybe 85%. But it was enough that they would have to decide what to do about protection. At least since they'd gotten home with the baby, they hadn't had time or energy for needing protection, but he was hoping soon. Very soon.

By the time she stormed back in the door, the baby was still sleeping, and he was picking up miscellaneous laundry lying around the house. It was like the baby shed clothes from one end to the other. All without the ability to do anything for himself. Though she slammed into the apartment, she quietly turned around and shut the door behind her, instantly spying the sleeping baby.

Thankfully, she didn't wake the baby. But she did have different shoes on than when she had left. These were a pair of nice black boots, but she had left in her house slippers. Which she didn't seem to notice on the way out.

"How was Ruth?" he asked her as she kicked off the boots by the door.

"Everybody was good," she said, still facing the wall and kicking the shoes, moving them so they were on the rug she kept there.

"Everybody?" he asked, and she stopped moving the boots.

He was sure he knew who everybody was, but why had she seen them all, he had no clue.

Shoes in place, she whipped around and said, "We have to talk."

"Yes, we do," he said, maybe a little too happily. She was bringing it up.

"You first." She glanced at the baby.

"We need a bigger place." He waved his hand at the room between them.

"Do *we*?" she asked, emphasizing the we part.

"Yes, we can't raise a baby in here. There's not enough room for three." He listed his first argument. Space and their need for more. Way more.

"But where would we go?" she asked, as if the apartment had been in her family for generations, and she couldn't imagine going anywhere.

"A house?" he asked tentatively. That was the logical place to go, but if there were other options, he was open to them.

"Do you have a house?" She moved toward the couch as she asked in case he had been hiding it from her all these months.

"No, but we would have to find one." He followed her as she went.

"Here?" She sounded like she couldn't even believe this was happening.

"Yes, in Landstad. We both work here."

"Are there any?" she asked, sitting on the couch.

"I don't know, I haven't looked yet. But there should be something out there."

"I enjoy living downtown. It's fun. Short commute. I thought Noah would play with Ruth's baby one day. I didn't even think it was too small." She leaned against the back cushion and looked at the ceiling.

"Don't you feel it's too small? Noah sleeps in the same room we eat in." He moved toward her.

"Maybe I just haven't gotten my bearings back after coming home. I mean, you were home weeks before me." She looked at all the stuff.

"You're not ready yet?" He sat on the couch beside her.

"I just need time. A lot has changed in a little time. Could we get rid of some stuff, and move in some of your stuff? For now," she said, looking at the room around her.

"Okay, we can try. I want my clothes here. Maybe by Spring, you will be yourself." He took her chin in his hand and kissed her lips.

Though he had only meant it to be a light kiss, she deepened it immediately and climbed onto his lap. When he slipped his hands under her shirt to cup her breasts, she moaned. "Make it quick; he'll be up soon."

With a growl, he pushed her away and said, "We have to stop."

Disappointment was etched onto her face when she asked, "Why? Is it because I haven't had real pants on all week? Is this a turn-off?" She waved her hands over her outfit that was adorable on her. More than adorable. Right down to her biting her lip.

Hating stopping her, hating the look on her face as he did it, he pulled back. "You're perfect, Nordskov, but you wanted to talk about something. We should do that before the baby wakes up."

"But it can wait. Talk when he is awake. Sex now." She started to pull her shirt off over her head.

"Nordskov," he said in a warning voice.

"Strong," she said in the same warning voice, and her shirt came off and hit him in the face.

"Now, talk." He held her shirt out to her, but she ignored it.

"Okay, okay." She bit her lip and folded her arms over her bare breasts, then her eyes met his. "Tess and Math are engaged."

"Really?" He tried to keep his eyes from her perfect breasts and failed.

"Yup, she asked him. He girlishly said yes." Amanda laughed on his lap.

"I would girlishly say yes, too." He tossed the shirt behind the couch. He didn't want her to have it back anymore.

Her laughter stopped, and she looked at him. "Do you want me to ask?"

He grinned at her. "Do you want to ask?"

"But what if you don't say yes?" She looked into his eyes.

"I was going to ask you at Christmas before I messed up. So, I would probably say yes." His hand slid up her arms and into her short blond hair.

"But we can't ruin their engagement." She slid her hands up his chest.

"We'll keep it a secret for a few months."

"But you hate keeping things a secret. Hence the breakup."

"I can spend time just enjoying you and our little secret. I have matured over the last few months. And your son has my name, so you're not going anywhere." He kissed her.

"I am so in love with the new you. Of course, I loved the old one too." She laughed.

"Nordskov." He pulled her closer to him. "I don't even remember not loving you."

"I like that." She kissed him.

"Mandy, I have something to say. The last day in the hospital, when I talked to David, it was because he wanted to tell me why I can't have kids. We had done some tests a few weeks before, and he had the results. Since Krystal wouldn't tell me why, I wanted to know." His hands ran down her side over her warm skin and held her hips.

"What did he say?"

"That my ex-wife lied to me. It was her, not me. So, we have to use protection now. I'm sorry, I—" Her words drained out anything he was going to say.

"You have known a week and didn't tell me?"

"Actually, I talked to Krystal on Sunday. Her answers confirmed that she had lied to me. Until then, I really didn't believe David."

Amanda pulled away and looked at him. "You knew, and you didn't tell me?"

"I am telling you now," he said, wishing he had just told her when he found out. Finally, he saw how easy it was to fall into an Amanda spiral.

Amanda groaned. "Now doesn't help me. Now?"

"What are you talking about?" he asked in confusion.

Instead of answering, she leaned into him and hugged him close to her, her face buried into his neck before she said, "How about this morning, when I was freaking out because I'm pregnant, and you can't have kids? How about then? When I thought you would leave and accuse me of cheating on you and hating me forever."

"Wait, you're pregnant again?" He cupped her face so that she was looking at him.

"Yes. I guess David should have told you earlier. Would have been good to know, you know, *earlier*." She bit her lip to stop the smile. He wasn't mad.

"How are you feeling? Are you nervous? Scared?"

"A little queasy in the mornings. A little nervous, but David thinks it was stress-related. And I'm making an appointment to see him ASAP, which is going to be awkward. But we can't take chances with baby Strong." She touched her stomach.

"Do we have to keep this one a secret?"

"No, this time, we tell the world. Just keep shush about us getting married." She put a finger to his mouth. He bit at it.

Across the room the baby made a noise, causing them both to look over at the crib. "Look Nordskov, you woke the baby."

"I did not. You're the one with the loud voice."

"You're the one with the adorably loud laugh."

"Don't blame me. I am innocent here."

"You are never innocent, Mandy," he whispered

Her eyes lit up. "You want me naked?"

He laughed. "I always want you naked, Nordskov. Always."

EPILOGUE

"I HAVE TO GO, HUE," Mandy whispered but knew it didn't sound genuine, even to her. Because it was all a lie. Hue had her pinned to the wall and was kissing her bare shoulder, heading south. Knowing where he was going made her never want to stop him.

Except they were in the church, in the little room where the wine was kept. Years ago, she had wished she had the nerve to come in here to try that wine. Now she wished she had the nerve to let Hue continue until the ache he had stirred up was extinguished. Which was a far worse activity than stealing a little cheap wine in this room.

"Nobody is stopping you, Nordskov." He nipped at the swell of her breast, making her gasp.

His hand was trying to find a way under her dress, which was going to be impossible because the shiny white fabric went all the way to the floor. With a frustrated groan, she helped him by lifting the fabric herself. After all, she was an independent woman who knew what she wanted and went for it.

Instantly, his hot hand was on her leg and snaking its way up. "Mandy, you look amazing in this dress, but I want it off you. Now."

"Too many buttons, we have to work around it." She pushed her chest in his hand, bodice and all. It had to be enough for now.

Tonight, she would let him take the dress off her any way he wanted, and that included ripping it from her body. Which was what he was planning, and that was before this little make out session even began.

Today was their long-awaited wedding day—if by long it meant two months, because that was how long the town had known they were engaged. Most of the actual wedding stuff had been planned by the book club and her mom since she was busy with the baby and getting back to work.

When they had first said they were getting married, the plan was a quick ceremony at the courthouse. But her mom wouldn't hear about it, saying they could just as easily get married at the church. Which was true.

Then the dress she wanted wasn't "wedding-looking" enough, so she, Kit, Julia, and their mom had gone dress shopping. Amanda was sure it was more for Kit, who was sure that Thomas would pop the question soon. Everyone was sure since they had bought a house recently, in Landstad, even if neither worked here or even planned to. This was their home.

It was only then that she just said yes to everything. She didn't have the energy to fight it, so she wasn't going to get her way.

After dropping the baby off with her mom, she had come up here to talk to Hue because she didn't believe they couldn't see each other before the wedding. In fact, she needed to see him. Even if she had woken up beside him, she needed to reassure herself this was real. And boy, it was real.

"Do you need these panties?" Hue's hand cupped her over the mentioned item.

In her head, she debated the actual need for them. Get married with a bare butt or with panties in front of the entire church. Nobody would know, right? "It's my good luck blue item."

Her words came too late as she felt the fabric tear from her body and his fingers replace fabric. Trying not to moan, she knew they didn't need luck to make this last forever; it was a sure thing.

"Try not to make noise, Nordskov." He sank to his knees between her legs.

"Holy fuck." It was exactly what she was going to say, but it was her brother saying the words from the door. Math's hand was already covering his eyes as he slammed the door shut.

Instantly, Hue dropped her dress and fell flat on his butt. Grabbing the shredded blue panties from the floor beside him, he shoved them in his pocket, grinning as he did it. "Try knocking, Math."

"We're in a church—keep your pants on." Math lowered his hand and scowled at them. "And with my sister. I should have killed you when I had the chance."

"Grow up, Math." Amanda straightened her dress and tried to act like her brother hadn't messed up the best part of the entire wedding. No matter how old he was, he would always be her stupid little brother. "You know that Hue and I have sex, live together, and have created a child together. And you are not one to talk. You got a woman you barely know pregnant. At least I knew Hue when he got me pregnant."

"I'm not listening to this. We had an agreement that I would never have to hear, or see for that matter, what happens between you two. In my mind, you have bunk beds."

"And who gets the top bunk, Math?" Hue asked in confusion.

"Mandy, because she would have called it the first night and never let anyone else have a turn."

"Don't worry, Math, Hue likes being on the bottom just as much as I enjoy being on top. But to make you feel better, just this morning, I let him be on top. He seemed happy, very happy." Mandy grinned at her brother, who slammed his hands to his ears and started to hum loudly.

"See you at the altar, Mandy." Hue kissed her, way more PG-13 since Math was in the room.

"I'll be there in white." She touched his cheek and couldn't wait to see him again, even if it would be in front of everyone.

Smiling, she headed out the back door and into the summer sunshine; the day had turned out gorgeous, not too hot, not too cold, and all sunny. As if her mom had ordered up the weather, which Dolly probably did.

Behind her, Math said quietly to Hue, "Why would you marry my sister? She's so annoying."

Hue laughed at his friend. "Because I love her."

Shutting the door, she couldn't stop grinning. Hue loved her, and in a few minutes, he was going to tell more than Math that. He was telling everyone.

Lifting her dress, she headed down the stairs. She needed to get to her own room of waiting, which was in the basement. Just like at every wedding, the bride was in the basement and the groom in the wine room. Not its actual name, but when you were raised in the church, it was the most important thing in the room.

Just as she hit the bottom step, she almost ran into her aunt Dotty and uncle Roger coming from their car. Roger didn't even look her way as they went, but Dotty stared at her and then looked up the steps. She knew exactly where Amanda had been.

Blushing, Mandy dipped her head and felt embarrassed for getting caught. As if her aunt knew exactly what they had been doing and that Amanda no longer had panties on.

Then she straightened. It didn't matter what her aunt thought of her. After all, everyone coming to the wedding—hell, everyone in the entire town—knew that she and Hue had already slept together. Mandy was visibly pregnant again. They were living together.

This time around, the depression she had felt throughout her pregnancy with Noah wasn't there. There wasn't even a hint of it. Which meant that it wasn't caused by her pregnancy, just her stupid decision to tell nobody about it.

"Morning, Dotty, Roger." She smiled politely at them.

"Morning, Amanda. Your dress is beautiful."

"I know." She touched the dress—it was gorgeous.

"Mandy, can you aim the bouquet at Mia today? I know Kit is probably going to be next, but Mia needs all the help she can get," Dotty whispered and looked around.

"Mia will find love when she finds love. A few roses tossed in the air won't help that." It was exactly how it had happened with her. Why hadn't she fallen for Hue her first day back in Landstad? It was a mystery, one she had stopped trying to solve. She loved him now, and that was all that counted.

Dotty just sniffed in annoyance as Roger opened the door of the church and let the two women in. Amanda ignored her aunt and headed to the basement, then to the room where she knew Mia was waiting for her. A short breastfeeding session had gone on long.

Mandy rushed into the room and looked Mia up and down in her peach dress. It was Mia's choice to wear the dress, but it did little for her. It just washed her out and made her look sad. "Look at you all lonely."

"I'm here with all my friends." Mia smiled, but it didn't reach her eyes.

"Then it's a good thing I came." Mandy jumped up beside her.

"Get down. You'll wrinkle your dress," Mia warned.

"I don't care; let it be wrinkled. I'm sitting with my favorite cousin." Mandy put her arm around her.

Mia's mom was pushing for her to get married, and Mia was feeling the pressure. But in a town like Landstad, single men were few and far between. With her words still ringing in Amanda's ears, she tried to tell her cousin that there was someone out there for her.

Mia smiled. "At least we will always be cousins."

"Does that mean that we won't have lunch once a week when we're old?" Like their moms did, Mandy didn't add.

"Probably not. You will get together with Kit and never have enough grandkids to beat her." Mia laughed.

"Kit wins all day long. I'll stick with you, though. We'll talk about our mom hips and have a competition to see who has more grandkids."

"You will win, no kids means no grandkids." Mia sighed.

"There's always Rafferty," Mandy said with a wink. She had never understood why they weren't a couple or even dated, not once. They were a cute couple who had a lot in common, but it seemed there was no spark, or something would have happened by now.

"No, that's over. Whatever it was," Mia admitted.

"Then there's someone out there for you."

"No, he was the one. Ever since high school, he was the one." Mia's words sounded so like all hope was gone.

"High school?"

"Yup."

"Why are you giving up so easily then?" If she was in love with Rafferty, shouldn't she fight for him? Mia had been there for everyone's rock bottom, and here she was, alone.

Amanda promised herself once this wedding was over, she was going to make sure her cousin got the man she wanted. And she wanted Rafferty Brooks, that was for sure.

Everyone was convinced she was being too picky, but she had already picked. She had just been waiting.

BONUS EPILOGUE

And she slept. His football-watching partner was sound asleep on the other end of the couch. She was at least wearing the correct jersey today, and so was the baby on her chest, who was also sleeping through the game. Today she hadn't even made it to kickoff, just dropped off to sleep the minute she sat down during the pregame. Not even her complaining about having to watch the pregame show kept her awake.

Not that Hue was complaining; he knew she was tired. So was the baby. He had been up half the night last night, and so had she. But neither of his parents were complaining about it today. Both were happy to give up a night's sleep for a day with their son. Amanda hadn't said a word about it this morning when he had woken up after only an hour of sleep to start his day.

He would get up and put the baby in his crib, but the baby in his arms was still awake. First, he would have to get Noah to sleep, then he could deal with Hudson. Eleven-month-old Noah was almost asleep, but he was still fighting it. He smiled at his son, whose blue eyes looked up at him—his mom's eyes. They would slowly fall closed and then pop open, just fighting it. But Hue and Noah had done this hundreds of times now, and he would soon give up and just sleep.

Unlike his baby brother, who was his mom's baby through and through. He slept every moment he got, except at night. At close to two months old, he still slept more than he was awake. Hue had thought Noah had been an easy baby, but it looked like his little red-headed boy was going to be even easier.

To the delight of his parents, Hudson had been born only one month early—after Amanda had been on bedrest for three months. And he had been born with red hair instead of the near-white hair of every other Nordskov baby. Amanda had been the first to see it, but she was an expert at babies. Now at two months, Hue could see it as well, though it was still very thin.

David had performed a C-section, and it had been slower and less dramatic than Noah's birth, but the results were the same: a healthy, breathing boy. Amanda had named him after Hue himself, just replacing the e with a d on hue son. Hudson. Not that it had mattered that his one was actually his. Noah was his firstborn no matter what.

Noah was finally sleeping, so Hue took him to the bedroom to put him in his crib. Slowly and silently, he walked through the apartment to what used to be Amanda's bedroom and put the baby in one of the two matching cribs in the room. Retrieving the tinier boy from his wife's chest, he put him in the other crib.

The apartment was still smaller than he would want to raise his sons, and if they chose to have another baby, they would run out of room fast. But they would be staying here. In March, they had bought the building from Ruth and had started renovating his old apartment to a master bedroom and office space for her. It had taken almost until Hudson's birth before Hue had finally finished it when she was on bedrest. So now their apartment was twice the size of what it was before, but it was still full of baby things. Hue figured it always would be.

But she loved just going downstairs to get to work. Hue usually took Noah to daycare down two blocks, and so far, Hudson hadn't been there yet. But soon, Amanda would go back to work. The town had finally realized while she was on maternity leave for Noah that there were enough people going to the clinic to hire another nurse practitioner and a receptionist, thus lightening the load for her.

In June, they had gotten married in a small ceremony at the church, then had a bigger reception for their family and friends. It was a good day, but it was the day he got Amanda, so anything could have happened, and he wouldn't have cared.

Sitting on the couch, he pulled her into his arms so he could have his wife sleeping on him instead of a baby. He really liked her the best. Sometimes he wished he had just asked her out the day she moved in, and they would have had an extra year. But he liked how it turned out, and he got Amanda Nordskov in the end.

Running his hand lightly over her hair, he smiled at his wife. He always loved sleeping with her. No matter what kind of sleeping with her it was.

ALSO BY ALIE GARNETT

<u>Landstad, ND</u>

<u>Invisible</u>

<u>Irresistible</u>

<u>Impulsive</u>

<u>Insuppressible</u>

<u>Intriguing</u>

<u>Imperfect</u>

<u>Irreplaceable</u>

<u>The Great Lovely Falls</u>

Falling for the Single Mom

Falling for his Best Friends Sister

Falling for the Boss

Falling for his Step-Sister

Falling for his Fake Wife

Falling into a Second Chance

<u>Hart Series</u>

Seeing her Pain

Her Favor

Max Valentine is Looking at Me!

Keeping her Safe

<u>Stand Alone</u>

Romancing the Doctor

ABOUT ME, ALIE GARNETT

I love to read and prefer a little spice in those books. I am lucky enough to live on a small hobby farm in northern Minnesota with her husband and two kids. I enjoy spending time in the pasture with my two mini horses and one fainting goat (who doesn't actually faint). When I'm not writing, I'm busy trying to do all the things I didn't get to while writing. Or maybe I wouldn't have gotten to them anyway, because its laundry, dishes and fun things like that.

www.ingramcontent.com/pod-product-compliance
Lightning Source LLC
Chambersburg PA
CBHW010543170726
48285CB00008B/2722